When A Door Closes

BARBARA M. LAMACCHIA

Double J Press
Berlin, Massachusetts

ISBN 978-1-7353479-9-8 (paperback)

ISBN 979-8-9903879-2-8 (ebook)

Library of Congress Control Number: 1-15055665051

For Dottie

*"When friendships are real,
they are not glass threads or frost work,
but the solidest things we can know."*

—Ralph Waldo Emerson

Contents

<h1 style="text-align:center">1989</h1>

Bridget "Bridy" Kerr surveyed the scene before her with incredulous eyes. The entire Kerr clan had gathered at a restaurant to celebrate her graduation from law school. As she sipped her wine, Bridget reflected on all that had happened during the time she spent at BC Law.

The most momentous incident involved her oldest brother John, the former mayor of their hometown. Three years previously, he had been involved in a car accident that claimed the life of a young woman, a reporter for the local daily, *The Clarion*. Pup, as his family called him, had been seriously hurt and was now in a wheelchair. He was charged with manslaughter in the young woman's death. However, all charges were dropped when the police investigation revealed that the weather had caused the accident, not driver error.

Many people thought the mayor had been given a sweetheart deal. The investigation had been labeled a sham, a whitewash, a miscarriage of justice. The family of the dead woman had filed a wrongful death suit, which was thrown out of court. Pup recovered enough that he was able to return to work at the building company that he had founded many years ago. Even though he broke two vertebrae, the former mayor remained convinced that he would someday walk again.

The mother of the Kerr clan, Theresa Kerr, died of a massive stroke in 1987. Her death was unexpected and had left her husband and children shocked and bereft. The oldest of the children, Mimi, along with her husband Neil, welcomed their eighth child, Liam Robert, into the world a mere two months after the matriarch's death.

But to Bridget's mind, the greatest tragedy of the past few years happened to her brother Dan aka Chip, who had been the managing editor of *The Clarion*. After the acquittal of the mayor of all charges in the fatal accident, Chip fired the entire editorial board after they had called the acquittal "The scandal of the century," implying that the mayor had gotten away with murder. *The Clarion's* parent company reinstated the board and fired Chip, who could not find employment at any other publication afterwards.

Bridget snapped back to reality when Chip stood up and proposed a toast to the sister, whom he called, "The most successful Kerr," proclaiming, "You've come a long way since you used to sit on the living room floor and color. You swam with the sharks in the corporate world in New York City only to return to your roots and totally reinvent yourself. Here's to Bridget Kerr, Esquire."

The family applauded and cheered, as did several other patrons in the restaurant. Despite her worldliness, Bridget felt herself blushing at her brother's effusive compliment. When she regained her composure, Bridget thanked Chip and the rest of the family, saying that all of them had helped her in their own ways during her three long years in law school. "We've certainly had our share of trouble and heartache, but here we are all together to celebrate my big day. I raise my glass to all of you."

Bridget had accepted a job at a local firm. She was only interested in civil law and wanted no part of corporate or criminal law, although Bridget was well aware that her work at the firm might involve some low-level criminal cases. More than anything, Bridget wanted to help working people, whether through drafting a will or helping a young couple to close on their first home. Altruism was ingrained in her by her parents, and she wanted to ensure that her clients would be treated fairly by the justice system.

Two aspirins and a generous cup of chamomile tea did little to relieve the pounding headache Bridget endured the evening of her first day of work at the firm. As much as she tried to forget the day, the events and images kept coming back to her; demons who would not give up torturing her. The day began with a welcome from the receptionist, not the senior partner. Valerie showed Bridget her office, a tiny space painted an institutional gray and hardly bigger than the walk-in closet had been in her Manhattan apartment. The office had a desk with a phone, a spartan chair, and a window that faced downtown Coltonwood. A stack of manila folders stood in the exact center of the desk, some more than an inch thick.

Bridget got to work examining the folders, which contained paperwork about open cases at the firm, the usual minutiae left to the newest associate to wade through and dispose of. Valerie interrupted mid-morning to inform Bridget that she had two appointments that afternoon.

"Are those cases among this stack?" Bridget asked.

"No. The people coming in are new clients. All we know are their names and phone numbers."

"When are they coming in?"

"The first appointment is at twelve-thirty. The next is at three."

Bridget planned to grab a sandwich at Zippy's since she had neglected to make herself lunch that morning. Before she could leave, Mr. Piersall, the senior partner, paid her a visit. He poked his ample head of snow-white hair into her office.

"Good morning, Bridget. I came to apologize for not meeting you this morning. I was tied up with some unexpected business."

"Good morning, Mr. Piersall. I understand," said Bridget, who strongly suspected the business was hardly unexpected, probably an early tee time.

"How has your morning been so far?"

"I'm pretty busy reading the cases I've been given. Valerie told me I have two appointments this afternoon."

The boss smiled. "That's fine. You might as well get right into the saddle. Carry on."

The first client was a middle-aged woman who plunked herself into a chair and informed Bridget that she expected her case to be handled with discretion and dispatch. The woman then went into a long diatribe about her son and how he had been victimized by the court system and her expectation that Bridget would rectify that situation. Bridget listened and took a few notes. At last, when the woman stopped speaking, Bridget asked for the age of her son, suspecting that he was a misguided teenager. She was astounded when the woman said her son was thirty-five. His latest offense was shoplifting at a local grocery store. Bridget wrote down the particulars of the case and sent the woman on her way.

The next client was a disgruntled older man who was hellbent on suing his former builder for some botched work on an addition to his house. According to the man, the builder had measured all the windows incorrectly, and now they were all different lengths and needed to be replaced. The client made it quite clear that he expected Bridget to force the builder to replace the windows and pay several million in damages. When Bridget offered several million dollars was excessive and unrealistic, the man yelled and pounded the desk. The yelling brought a worried Valerie to Bridget's office. "It's okay, Valerie. Mr. Seaver is just making sure I understand his position."

"Damn right. You'd better understand my position. I know my rights, and I will have them."

Again, Bridget made some notes and sent her still angry client away. Bridget ignored her growling stomach and returned to the stack on her desk. She was still reading when Valerie appeared in the doorway and wished her good night.

"How was your day?" asked the affable receptionist.

"Hectic, and I still have to finish reading all this material."

"Forget it. Go home. The stack will still be there tomorrow."

Such was Bridget's first day as an associate at Piersall, Gallarani, and Ryan. She was astounded at how tired she was. Even when she was commuting twenty-plus miles to Boston twice a day to law school, she hadn't felt such fatigue. Bridget wondered if she had made the right choice when she went to law school.

The next morning, Valerie informed Bridget that Mr. Piersall would like to see her in his office as soon as possible. Bridget couldn't imagine what he wanted as she walked to the opulent office on the other side of the building.

"Good morning, Miss Kerr. Please take a seat."

"Good morning, Mr. Piersall." She waited for her boss to speak.

"What happened yesterday during your meeting with Mr. Seaver? He called me last night and complained that you were unprofessional and rude."

An astounded Bridget faced her employer. "That's not how it was, Mr. Piersall. Mr. Seaver became belligerent and loud when I told him that the damages he sought were unrealistic and excessive. He started yelling and pounding my desk. Now you tell me who was rude."

Mr. Piersall sat back in his deeply padded chair. "I see. Thank you for giving me the other side of the story. That will be all. Have a good day."

Bridget went back to plowing through the case files on her desk. The ringing of the phone startled her.

"Hey, Bridy, it's your favorite brother."

"Hi, Pup. Why are you calling me at work? Has something happened?"

"Nothing bad. I found an apartment for you."

"But I didn't ask you to find an apartment for me."

"No, but I know you want to live on your own, and I know about this place. It's a two-bedroom apartment in an old house on Pleasant St. I just happen to be the owner. What do you say? Do you want to look at it?"

"Sure, but I can't until Saturday."

"That's fine. Do you want to go to breakfast first?"

"Absolutely. I'll meet you at Friendly's at eight thirty. Is that okay?"

"Perfect. See. I told you I'm your favorite brother."

* * * * * *

Pup was already seated at a table sipping coffee when Bridget arrived.

"How did you get here so fast?"

"I'm always way ahead of you."

Bridget smirked. "That'll be the day. I still can't believe you found an apartment for me."

"I figured it's time you had your own place, and now that you have a steady job, you can afford to live on your own. I think you'll like it."

"How much is the rent?"

"Five hundred a month, but that includes heat. You won't find a bargain like that anywhere else."

"What if I don't like it?"

"Then you're on your own."

After they ordered, Pup casually mentioned that he got a play-by-play description of Bridget's first day at the law firm.

"Where did you hear that?"

"From old man Seaver himself."

"That's outrageous. All of that is supposed to be confidential. How well do you know this guy?"

"I know him somewhat. His father used to own a restaurant in town before our time, in the thirties and forties. Eventually, he sold the business, and Chet inherited the dough from the sale, and he's been living off his father's fame ever since."

"How do you know all this?"

"I make it my business to know as much as I can about Coltonwood. Dad would remember old man Seaver and the restaurant. The son bought quite a bit of real estate with his inheritance, so he thinks he's among the elite of the city. He's a lightweight with a big mouth."

"I guess so. The less I see of him, the better."

Pup then rambled on about some other old timers in Coltonwood. Her brother's knowledge of the town and its inhabitants amazed Bridget. He seemed to know everyone, old and young. No wonder he won his two terms as mayor in landslides.

Bridget admired her oldest brother despite his many faults. Since his accident, Pup had become far more tolerant and patient. His persistence and refusal to give in or give up during his convalescence was nothing less than inspiring. Pup still had his gift of gab, and his knowledge of Coltonwood and its history was encyclopedic.

"Well, shall we go and see the apartment?"

"What apartment?"

At Bridget's confused look, Pup jeered, "Ha. Gotcha. Did you think I forgot?"

Chapter 2

The apartment was perfect for Bridget. She had plenty of room but not much furniture. In her apartment in New York City, she had the essentials but little else, all of which she left behind when she moved out. She was amazed that she had managed to live five years with little or no furniture save for a bed and a kitchen table with one chair. She missed the familiar comfort of her family home, but she relished the privacy of her own place.

Bridget converted a bedroom into a home office complete with a brand-new Mac, a huge contraption which took up an inordinate amount of space on her desk. When she started the new job, Bridget had decided she would not take work home, but she could not keep that promise. There was simply not enough time during the day to meet with clients and handle the paperwork that had doubled since she began work at Piersall, Gallarani, and Ryan. Bridget foolishly thought she would have extra time to read the books that had been piling up beside her bed, but she was too tired at night to read. She also found, to her surprise, that in her few idle moments she was lonely. She missed the easy familiarity of living with her father and the constant coming and going of her siblings, nieces, and nephews. Bridget had lost contact with her friends in New York and had not reconnected with her high school or college friends. Her friends from BC Law were in the same predicament as she, with too much work and too little free time.

Bridget's brother Chip had become her closest friend and confidant. Chip had plenty of time on his hands since he had been relieved of his duties at *The Clarion*, the local newspaper. Chip had been unemployed for a few months until he found a part-time job teaching journalism at a community college. The Kerr family provided plenty of fodder for conversation. Occasionally, the patriarch would drop by on a weekend, sometimes accompanied by their outrageous neighbor, Mrs. Salina. During one such visit, Bridget mentioned she was lonely and restless when she wasn't occupied with legal matters.

"Why don't you get a cat?" Chip suggested. "They're good company and not a lot of work."

Bridget never considered getting a pet of any kind. The Kerr family never had pets, and Bridget never entertained the idea of getting one.

"Or," Chip continued, "you could get a rattlesnake; not much work there. Or maybe get a parrot or a lizard. I could teach a parrot to talk. Now that would liven up your life."

Her oldest brother, Pup, was also a frequent visitor. Bridget and Pup, who was a decade older, had never been close, but since his accident, Pup had often sought Bridget's company. Pup was also her landlord, so she saw him at least once a month. Bridget often thought of her life in New York; a life that was consumed by work. Even when she saw her friends socially, their conversations always revolved around the all-consuming world of fashion design. Life in New York had been a whirlwind. Bridget couldn't fathom now how she had lasted for five years caught in that maelstrom.

After weeks of dealing with impatient clients, frustrating old cases, and general legal mania, Bridget was ready for some 'me time' to clear her head and get away from Coltonwood, if only for an afternoon. She got up early on Saturday morning and headed west with no specific destination in mind. Western Massachusetts was gorgeous in the fall, a panorama of color. This day's brilliant blue sky stood in sharp relief against the reds and golds that lined the Mass Pike. Bridget exited the pike just beyond Springfield in search of coffee and an apple spice donut, which she soon found at an apple orchard teeming with people.

She waited ten minutes to buy her coffee and donut, which she carried to a small table near a window. As she ate, she watched the people, mostly families, as they happily consumed coffee, cider and donuts. Soon her people watching gave way to a pang of loneliness, a sense of not belonging. Bridget finished her donut and took her coffee, surrendering her table to a young couple with a baby.

The morning sun had given way to clouds that promised rain. Instead of continuing west as she intended, Bridget headed back towards home. As she drove, she thought of her siblings and pondered their relationships.

Her oldest sister, Mimi, and her husband, Neil, had the most stable marriage. Mimi relished her role as the mother of eight. She was the most like their mother, the late matriarch of the Kerr clan. Like her mother, Mimi never worked outside her home once she married. She was content and happy, in sharp contrast to Cissy, the mother of two sons, who was known for her hysterics over nothing and constant fault-finding. Bridget wondered how on earth Cissy's husband Carl lived with her. Pup's marriage to Elaine had survived Pup's numerous infidelities, a nearly fatal heart attack, and a devastating accident that claimed a life and left Pup paralyzed. Through all of that, Elaine had remained steadfast and even quit her job to take over Pup's business. Bridget could only marvel at Elaine's selflessness. Gabby's pseudo-marriage to Stanley was risible, but Gabby was too insecure and too proud to leave Stanley, whom Bridget regarded as a drunk and a clown. Chip and Rosalina's marriage seemed to be on a solid footing. Both were stable people who loved and respected each other. Bridget did not know the stability of her younger sister Biddy's marriage to Dexter, but they seemed happy and content, both occupied with their careers.

By the time Bridget arrived back in Coltonwood, a drenching rain was falling, and her mood matched the weather. Why was she bothering to analyze her siblings' lives? They were all adults and, in every case but one, older than her. Their lifestyles were their own business. So intent had she been on her thoughts that Bridget forgot her coffee until it was stone cold. There was nothing to be done now except to return to her apartment and pour herself a generous glass of Cabernet and watch the rain fall.

* * * * * *

Often Bridget wondered if she had chosen the wrong profession. She didn't dread going to work, but the law didn't satisfy her as much as she thought it should. Swamped with work, she frequently stayed after her colleagues left for the day. To her surprise, Bridget enjoyed having the office to herself. She relished the quiet after the controlled chaos of the day with all the ringing phones and coming and going of clients. Sometimes Bridget would slip out and get takeout, which she would eat as she reviewed her cases. The unexpected ringing of her phone one such evening made her jump.

"Hello, Bridget?" screamed a familiar voice.

" Aunt Julia?"

"Yes. I'm so glad I caught you."

"Why are you calling? Is everything all right?"

"Fine. I just wanted to ask you to lunch on Thursday."

"I can do this Thursday, but I only have an hour for lunch."

"You can take another hour. If old man Piersall doesn't like it, tell him he can tuck it up his ass and fly."

Bridget loved Aunt Julia's sallies, but this one caught her totally off guard. So much so that once she started laughing, she couldn't stop. Once she caught her breath, she bid Aunt Julia good night.

On Thursday, Ramona, Aunt Julia's caregiver, drove Aunt Julia to the restaurant, so she was already seated when Bridget arrived.

"You beat me, I see," was Bridget's greeting as she gave Aunt Julia a peck on the cheek.

"Of course, I usually manage to beat everyone at everything. This drink is superb. Why don't you get one?"

"I can't drink. I have to go back to the office."

"The hell with the office. A cozy libation will relax you and help you think. Old man Piersall all but invented the three-martini lunch. Did you know that?"

"Not quite, Aunt Julia. A ginger ale will suit me just fine."

Bridget watched Aunt Julia closely. The nonagenarian's hand shook as she raised her glass, but she didn't spill a drop. Her eyes were filmy and slightly wet. An occasional raspy cough shook her emaciated frame. Aunt Julia glanced around the room, sometimes turning her body completely around to stare at another table.

"What are you having, Aunt Julia?" Bridget repeated the question when Aunt Julia failed to respond.

"What? What did you say?"

"What are you having?"

"I have a vodka martini."

"No. I mean to eat."

"I want the biggest steak they have."

The waiter brought Bridget's ginger ale and attempted to take their food order. Bridget ordered a chef's salad. Aunt Julia kept turning the menu over, much to the frustration of the busy waiter, whom Aunt Julia pinned with her deadly stare. "I want a steak."

"You mean our steak bomb sandwich?"

"What? A bomb? Why the hell would I want a bomb?"

"That's just the name of the sandwich, Aunt Julia."

"Would you like our pepper steak instead?' suggested the flustered waiter.

"You don't put pepper on steak. What's the matter with you? You should know that. I want a porterhouse steak, medium rare."

"I'm sorry, madam, but we don't offer a porterhouse steak."

"What? What kind of place is this that doesn't have steak? I demand to speak to the manager."

A few minutes later, a young man who looked about fifteen appeared and addressed Aunt Julia. "You had a question, ma'am?"

"I want to know why this place doesn't have steak. I never heard of such a thing."

The manager politely explained that the restaurant only offered sandwiches and salads, not dinner entrees.

"What? Sandwiches and salads? What kind of place is this? My niece here is a lawyer. I could have her sue the pants off you and the owner. Bring me another drink."

Bridget wished the floor would open up and swallow her. Several other diners overheard the exchange between Aunt Julia and the manager and were openly amused, but Bridget was not. "Aunt Julia, there is no reason for you to be so rude. The place doesn't serve dinner. Why not just get a salad?"

"I never eat salad," replied an unrepentant Aunt Julia. "During World War II, there was a meat shortage, but that was a few years ago. There's plenty of meat now."

When the waiter brought Aunt Julia's drink, Bridget asked him to bring the steak bomb sandwich minus the bread, hoping that it would placate Aunt Julia. The restaurant was busy, and the food was slow in coming. Bridget knew she had already used all of her lunch hour. She could only afford to stay for another fifteen or twenty minutes, but Aunt Julia was thoroughly enjoying her drink and in no hurry. When the food finally came, Bridget bolted half her salad, but Aunt Julia didn't even touch her food.

"Aunt Julia, I'm sorry, but I have to get back to work. Are you going to eat?"

The elderly lady looked blankly at Bridget. "I'll eat it later. I'm not in the mood for steak."

"Aunt Julia, will you excuse me? I have to make a phone call."

"Piersall, Gallarani, and Ryan. Valerie speaking. How may I direct your call?"

"Valerie, it's me, Bridget. Listen, I'm at a restaurant with my elderly aunt. I don't know when I'll be able to get back. Has anyone been looking for me?"

"Hi, Bridget. I'm sorry to say that no one has been looking for you. Partners one and two are out of the office. Partner three is stuck in his office. He's had a parade of clients all day. Will you be back before three? That's when I expect one and two to return."

"I'll make sure I'm back by then. Thanks, Valerie."

Bridget had a sudden thought. She called her brother, Chip, and prayed that he would pick up. He did as she was about to hang up.

"Chip, thank God. Do you have Ramona's number? I need to call her to pick up Aunt Julia. We're at Sully's, and I need to get back to work, but Aunt Julia's enjoying her second drink. You know how that is."

"I'll do better than that," replied Chip." I'll pick her up myself. Give me ten minutes."

"Thanks, Chip. You're a prince."

True to his word, Chip arrived and made an effusive show of greeting Aunt Julia as though by accident. Bridget paid the bill and apologized to the waiter and the manager for Aunt Julia's peevishness. Chip wheeled Aunt Julia into the parking lot just as Ramona pulled in. Because Aunt Julia had had two drinks, Chip didn't trust her steadiness, so he picked her up and placed her in the front seat of Ramona's car.

"I'll follow you and take her out the same way," Chip told Ramona. "She's not very steady on her feet."

Bridget hurried back to the office and prayed she would not encounter one of the partners. She didn't. Once inside the office, she took off her coat and glanced at her desk, where half a dozen phone messages awaited her.

Chapter 3

Bridget surveyed her apartment, arms akimbo, and shook her head, dismayed by the starkness of the space. The walls were beige and bare, and the few pieces of furniture placed at angles made the room look even smaller. She had to do something about the place. It was as bleak and uninviting as a hospital waiting room. Bridget had little experience in living-room decor. Family pictures, but nothing else, ornamented her family home. Her mother considered knick-knacks dust collectors not worth her time to keep clean. Bridget's apartment in New York didn't need any ornamentation since it was a place to sleep and shower, nothing else. But this apartment was Bridget's home, and she needed to make it feel like one.

Bridget fished some cash out of a drawer, picked up her coat and then balked. She hated shopping, an aversion that developed during her teen years when she had to do the food shopping at a nearby small grocery store. She and her younger sister Biddy would have to buy the family's groceries because their mother was unable to complete even the most basic of tasks, in stark contrast to the woman who had previously cooked every night for ten people. Bridget remembered going with her mother when she shopped for the enormous amount of food it took to feed such a large family. In those days, Theresa Kerr would bustle about the kitchen in her ubiquitous apron cooking, baking, or serving. She made her own bread, Parker House rolls, muffins, cakes, and pies. The family never had the same meal two nights in a row. Bridget and her siblings loved lamb chops, ham, chicken, steak, mashed potatoes, even carrots. By unanimous agreement, the Saturday night meal of hot dogs and homemade baked beans was the family's favorite.

Then everything changed. Her brother Champ went MIA in Vietnam.

Bridget was a junior in high school when that cataclysmic event occurred. Her older siblings were married or attending college. She and Biddy were the only Kerr kids living at home. Champ's disappearance was an earthquake that shook the solid foundation of the Kerr family. Theresa Kerr could hardly function. She stopped cooking and cleaning. Some days she never got out of bed. On other days she moped about in a robe and slippers and sat zombie-like in front of the TV. Bridget did the family's laundry, warmed up frozen dinners, changed the bed linens and basically ran the household. Mr. Kerr helped when he could, but he worked six days a week at his business.

Bridget had desperately wanted to escape this life and applied to out-of-state schools where she hoped to find a more normal existence. She felt guilty because her father depended on her so much. In the end, she attended the same community college that Mimi and Cissy had. Bridget knew she would not find peace by running away. She was also reluctant to leave Biddy, who, although only a freshman, was drinking and dabbling with drugs as her means of escape. If Bridget left home, Biddy would certainly be a lost soul.

Bridget hated these flashbacks, which could be triggered by the slightest thought or memory. Just putting cash into her wallet to buy some accessories for her apartment plunged her into the past, an abyss she tried daily to forget. She recalled how her brother Chip retreated into a journal he kept as a child whenever the past assailed him. Chip also had nightmares about Champ, a fate that Bridget had escaped. Some memories made her angry, such as when her boyfriend asked why her mother was never around when he was at the house. The memory of her senior prom rankled more than most because her mother never bothered to get out of bed to see Bridget in her gown. There was no graduation party for Bridget as there had been for each of her older siblings. Her mother did attend the graduation but took to her bed immediately after the ceremony.

Bridget often wondered what adolescence was like for her older siblings. Had Mum taken an interest in their activities? Did she go to school events or games? Had she taken pictures of Mimi, Cissy, and Gabby on their prom nights? Bridget knew that her mother would never attend a football game when Pup and Champ played. She said she was too nervous to watch, and what if one of the boys got hurt? Chip didn't play sports, and Bridget wondered what he did since he wasn't a jock. On a sudden whim, Bridget called Chip and invited him for a drink on Saturday afternoon. To her surprise, he readily agreed to come.

After she extended the invitation, Bridget realized she had nothing in her apartment to give Chip to eat or drink. She made a quick trip to the store for beer, wine, cheese and crackers. Why, she wondered for the fiftieth time, was her life away from work so boring? Bridget pondered inviting her father but soon dismissed the thought. Tonight would be a conversation between two Kerr "kids" free from parental interference.

Chip arrived toting beer and pretzels and ready to talk. He settled himself on the couch as though he lived there. He didn't seem surprised by this unexpected summons from his younger sister.

"How's life in the legal world?" was his opening remark.

"I like my job, but legal work can be dull and rather mundane. I spend a lot of time reading and researching. But I have met a lot of interesting people. Working with the clients is the best part."

"Are you in the courtroom a lot?"

"Not really. I do plenty of real estate work along with wills and trusts. None of that needs to be done in the courtroom. If you don't mind, I'd rather not discuss my work. The reason I invited you is because I want to ask you what you did when you were in high school."

Chip reached for some cheese and crackers and took a long drink from his beer. "Why are you interested in that? High school is so remote to me now. I remember my years at St. Tom's better than my high school years."

"But what did you do if you didn't play sports?"

"I definitely was not a jock. Pup and Champ lived and breathed sports. I was the boring brother who wrote for the school paper. I had a part in the senior play. I can't even remember the title of the play. It was something by Woody Allen, I think."

Bridget laughed. "How could you forget the title of a play you acted in?"

"I wasn't the lead by any means. I had a bit part with about five lines."

"Did Mum go see the play?"

"Of course. Mum and Dad went. So did you and Biddy, who didn't have a choice in the matter. You were dragged so Mum and Dad didn't have to get a babysitter."

"Did you do anything else?"

"I know you're a lawyer, but are you practicing the art of cross-examination on me?"

"No, I've been thinking lately about how miserable my high school years were. Mum had no interest in anything that I did. She spent most of her time in bed or dragging around the house in a robe and slippers. I could have painted the walls red, and she wouldn't have noticed or cared. I was lonely and angry in high school. I hated it when other girls mentioned doing things with their mothers. I had no idea what that was like. So, I just wondered what life was like for you in high school."

Chip was silent for a few moments and reached for another beer before he spoke. "I'm really sorry that you had such a bad time. It's a miracle you've done as well as you have, all things considered. What about Biddy? I presume she had a tough time too?"

"I think it was worse for Biddy. Her escape was drugs and alcohol, and Mum had no clue that Biddy was using and drinking. Imagine. If not for Dad, I shudder to think what would have become of Biddy. I'd like to ask her, but I'm sure she would rather forget those sad memories."

Chip slumped low on the couch. "Yeah, it was no fun being a Kerr kid once Champ disappeared. No fun at all."

Bridget kept thinking about Chip's parting words after their impromptu get together, "Once Champ disappeared, it was no fun being a Kerr kid." After seeing Chip, Bridget decided it was time to seek out some of her other siblings. As it happened, she had to visit a homebound client and would pass right by Pup's business. On her way back to the office, Bridget had time to stop and see Pup and Elaine.

Prime Builders, Pup's business, was on the outskirts of Coltonwood. It was simply a small building surrounded by dump trucks and other construction vehicles and equipment. The place was rather desolate and appeared deserted. A ramp to facilitate Pup's wheelchair fronted the building.

Bridget saw Elaine at her desk. She was on the phone and gestured for Bridget to sit. Pup was nowhere in sight. The office wasn't much bigger than Bridget's at the law firm. There were two desks side by side, a copy machine, two chairs for visitors, and a tiny bathroom to one side, which was much too small to accommodate Pup's wheelchair.

Elaine hung up and smiled at Bridget. "This is a pleasant surprise. What brings you here?"

"I had to see a client close to here, so I thought I'd stop in and chat for a minute. Where's Pup?"

"He's home."

"Is he sick?"

"No, he isn't sick. Usually, he's only able to work in the mornings. He gets tired easily and can't concentrate for too long. I close the office at noon, and we go home for lunch. I go back for the afternoon, but John has to stay home and rest."

Elaine's words troubled Bridget. Pup had always been a workhorse. He would put it many hours of overtime both as a businessman and as the mayor. It was inconceivable that he could only work for a few hours every day. It was as though Pup was a mere figurehead in the business he founded, his presence at the office more symbolic than necessary.

Bridget looked carefully at Elaine and didn't miss the worry lines around her eyes, the drawn look on her face.

"I thought Pup could do a lot more than he obviously does."

"The truth is, Bridy, that John cannot do much. He takes care of the mail, he signs purchase orders, answers the phone, and deals with contractors. He can't go to job sites; he's stuck here. He loves to talk on the phone and to negotiate with contractors. I think it reminds him of when he was mayor. Otherwise, he's clearly bored being here, and his fatigue catches up with him pretty quickly. I have to keep the books and make sure the guys get paid. Luckily, I was an office manager before I got married, so I was able to step in and take over the business."

Bridget had no real concept of Pup's business other than knowing he built housing developments and managed some rental properties. What would have happened if Elaine had not been able to take over and step into the breach after Pup's accident?

"I'm sorry, Elaine. I did not know that Pup wasn't able to run the business as he always had."

Elaine's smile was wistful. "I wish things were different, but this is the reality. I expect there will be no more business in a few years. Building has slowed down, and John's extracurricular activities haven't helped matters. I want him to sell now, but John won't hear of it. We're losing money, and we've had to lay off some workers. If not for the rental income, the business would be forced to close."

As Bridget listened to her sister-in-law, she wondered how on earth Pup and Elaine paid for their palatial home and its upkeep. Their bills for heat and electricity must be enormous, not to mention the mortgage payment. Obviously, Pup's indiscretions had ruined his life and livelihood and put a substantial burden on Elaine. The once powerful mayor was reduced to a man who stood to lose everything he had worked his whole life to create.

Bridget fretted about Pup and Elaine's circumstances as she drove back to the office. As a lawyer, she dealt with bankruptcies and foreclosures. Perhaps she could help Pup and Elaine before it was too late.

When Bridget returned to the office, she had little time to brood over Pup and Elaine's situation. She had a meeting with a disgruntled client who was incensed that his neighbor's tree had fallen on his property and the neighbor refused to pay for its removal. Bridget patiently explained to the man that even though the tree wasn't his, he was legally responsible to pay the removal expenses. The man was adamant that he would not pay. Bridget, frustrated and tired, asked Valerie to find the law that pertained to fallen trees and showed the statute to the client.

While she was engaged in legalities, Bridget's mind was focused totally on the law. Once the enraged client left, Bridget returned to her office, swallowed two aspirin, and thought again about Pup and Elaine. As a lawyer, she had learned to keep a professional distance, to avoid any emotional involvement with clients. Even when she lost a case, she still got paid, unlike Pup and Elaine, who owned their own business and whose whole lives revolved around it. They were fully invested and must remain so.

Bridget frequently toiled late at Piersall, Gallarani, and Ryan mostly due to the fact that her social life outside of work was nonexistent. As she worked on the fallen tree case, her mind kept wandering to the afternoon that she had spent with her brother Chip and how pleasant that had been. Bridget resolved to get in touch with all her other siblings and invite them to her apartment, which most of them had never seen. She called each one and invited them to her apartment for drinks and snacks the following Saturday. Mimi accepted, as did Pup, Cissy and Chip. Gabby waffled and said she had to check with Stanley. Biddy never returned her call. Then she called her father, who told her he was busy that night. "I'm taking Bernice to dinner." was his explanation. Bridget, rendered inarticulate by this pronouncement, could only utter, "Oh."

"I'd be glad to come some other time, but Saturday night is out."

"Oh."

Bridget bid her father goodbye and immediately rang Chip. "Who is Bernice?"

"Who?"

"Bernice. Dad's taking someone named Bernice to dinner next Saturday. Does Dad have a secret girlfriend?"

Chip replied, "I have no idea who Bernice is or if Dad has a girlfriend. I'll see what I can find out and let you know."

Bridget's legal mind gave her no peace, and she called Pup, who knew everyone in Coltonwood.

"Pup, does Dad have a lady friend named Bernice? Do you know who she is?"

"The only Bernice in town is Bernice Kirby. She ran Bernice's Braid Shop downtown. The beauty parlor was a few doors down from Dad's store. Do you remember that? She and Dad knew each other for sure. Are they an item now?"

"I don't know. That's why I called you."

"I was the mayor, not the town crier, yet inquiring minds still seek me out, so I'm glad that you called. I will investigate and let you know."

By the day of the get-together, all the Kerr "kids" were reeling, blindsided by the news that their father did indeed have a lady friend. When she wasn't at the office, Bridget lived in a haze, her mind a cauldron of mixed emotions. One minute she was happy, the next confused, the next angry. She had never imagined that her father would be interested in any woman other than Theresa Kerr. Bridget was anxious to find out if her siblings' reactions were similar to hers.

Once everyone had settled, Bridget could contain herself no longer. "I can't believe that Dad has a lady friend. What if they get married? She'd be our stepmother. I just can't imagine."

Mimi, the oldest, spoke first. "I think it's nice that Dad has someone. He went through a lot with Mum. He deserves to be happy again."

Cissy spoke up. "Where's Gabby? Why isn't she here?"

Bridget explained, "She couldn't come because Stanley wasn't available to watch the kids. He's such a sleazeball. He won't even stay with the kids so Gabby can get out for a few hours. He's despicable."

Chip chimed in, "I knew that when I first met Stanley, but no one believed me. He ingratiated himself to Mum and Dad and totally bamboozled Gabby."

"I wonder when we'll get to meet Bernice," Cissy asked. "I'll bet she's a gold digger who'll steal all of Dad's money, and none of us will get a cent. What if he leaves the house to her? I don't like this at all."

"Cissy, you seriously need to get a life," thundered Pup. "You're a selfish person. You always have been. You don't care whether or not Dad's happy. All you care about is getting your share of the inheritance. Your hair's always on fire about something. You're never happy with anyone or anything."

Cissy rounded on Pup. "Who are you to talk? You cheated on your wife, and you killed someone besides. You belong behind bars, and you would be if you weren't in a wheelchair."

"All right, Cissy. That's enough." Mimi's attempt to silence Cissy fell on deaf ears.

"Everyone in this family treats me like a second-class citizen. No matter what I do, I get criticized. No one respects my opinion. Every time we're all together, you all gang up on me. I'm sick of it."

Pup, red-faced, screamed, "And we're all sick of you, you whining hussy. Why don't you move to California and get yourself a New Age therapist who'll tell you to bathe in eucalyptus oil to solve all your problems? By the way, I never killed anyone. Laura died in an accident. If you had a sliver of a brain, you would know that."

Bridget had had enough. "This is ridiculous. Stop all this badmouthing, or I'll throw every one of you out." The hostess looked around helplessly. The counselor at the law did not know how to stop this domestic squabble among her older siblings. She needed to find a solution, and fast.

Everyone else looked down at their plates. No one wanted to make eye contact with anyone else. The silence was even more unnerving than the quarreling, as unsettling as that had been. Chip spoke first.

"Everyone needs to calm down," Chip said as he surveyed the room. "Every time we're together, we end up in a screaming argument. Think for a minute. Does it really matter if Dad has a lady friend? Is it the end of the world? No, it isn't. Dad has the right to do whatever he chooses, whether we approve or not. He doesn't need our permission to live his life his way."

"But," Cissy tried to interrupt, but Chip ignored her. "Truth be told, we should all mind our own business and leave Dad alone. He raised eight kids. I think he can manage very well without our guidance or advice."

"Bravo! Great speech, Chip," Pup jeered. "You ought to run for mayor. But I beg to differ. This is our business. If Dad falls for this woman, it will have repercussions for all of us. What do we know about this woman? Answer, nothing. What if she is after Dad's money, as our esteemed sister Cissy pointed out a few minutes ago? What if she makes Dad change his will? What if she insists Dad sell the house and move to Florida? We need to consider all of these possibilities."

"Is it really necessary to paint this doomsday scenario, Pup?" asked Mimi. "All we know is that Dad is taking a lady out to dinner. That's it. What's the big deal? You're all making it sound as though she's ready to move into the house and put her name on the deed. Why don't we all just take a deep breath and have another drink? If nothing else, let's have some consideration for Bridy. She invited us here to enjoy each other's company, as difficult as that is for some of us."

A tenuous peace ensued, but not for long.

Cissy looked at Bridget. "Bridy, did you make this dip or buy it?"

Sensing a trap, Bridget smiled and said, "Why do you ask? Do you really want to know, or are you trying to insult me?"

Incredulous, Cissy replied, "Why are you so sensitive? I just asked a simple question. Of course, you have the option not to answer."

Pup spoke up. "Don't bother answering, Bridy. Cissy's an idiot, and nothing you say will change that."

Bridget wished that the floor would open up and swallow her. After Pup's caustic remark, uncomfortable glances were exchanged, but no one spoke. The tension in the room was palpable, like the fission between thunder and lightning. For lack of anything else to do, Bridget looked out her front window and saw her neighbor playing touch football on the front lawn with his kids. She turned abruptly as Mimi spoke, "I'm leaving right now, and I think the rest of you should do likewise. After all we've been through as a family, we should be able to have a civil discussion without name-calling and backbiting. I shudder to think what Mum would say if she heard and saw the way we treat each other. Bridy, you can keep the brownies."

The door closed, but no one else moved or spoke. Bridget felt sweat at the base of her hairline as she pondered how to handle this situation. She considered a few curt remarks, but all she could manage was, "Does anyone want coffee?" No one answered or moved. Pup sat slumped in his wheelchair, a bear of a man confined to a movable prison. Cissy and Chip sat on the couch. Cissy appeared to study a picture on the wall, while Chip looked morosely at the floor. Bridget stared at the coffee cake she had bought that morning that no one had touched. She closed her eyes and tried to imagine herself in the courtroom speaking on behalf of a client. Still, no words came. A glacial age later, Pup said, "Chip, can you help me get out?"

Chip rose. "I'll help, but not until you apologize to Bridy. She went to a lot of trouble, and we spoiled her party, big time."

Pup executed an about-face in his chair and wheeled himself to the door. "Never mind. I can manage on my own. I think everyone should apologize, not just me."

"You can't get the chair beyond the step without help, Pup. Stop being so obstinate and petty," Chip responded.

Pup looked at his brother. "If you can hold the back, I can ease my way down the step."

Chip did as Pup asked and helped Pup get his chair down the one small step out of Bridget's apartment. Cissy wordlessly gathered up her coat and purse and followed her brothers out the door.

Chapter 4

Bridget suffered over this terrible debacle for several days. She was like an automaton who sleepwalked through her tasks at work, her head able to do what needed to be done but her heart shattered in the aftermath of the family gathering. Bridget wasn't even able to clean her apartment until the remnants of the party began to smell. Mimi's brownies were rock hard. The chips were rubbery and had to be discarded. Beer cans and wine bottles had to be rinsed and disposed of. Bridget did it all in a fog; her arms and legs attended each task, but her heart and mind were closed.

Work proved to be her only solace. She stayed at the firm long after everyone else had left. The silence of the office afforded cold comfort, but comfort nevertheless. The discipline Bridget learned in law school helped her to focus on the work that needed to be done, and she could parry her thoughts of family and concentrate only on legal matters. So absorbed was she in her work that one night she didn't leave the office until ten thirty.

At night, Bridget tossed and turned, her obsessive thoughts running like a movie through her mind. Even as a teenager, she had not been so overwhelmed by such feelings of remorse and dread. The few hours of sleep she eked out each night brought little relief to her troubled mind. A week later she phoned her sister Biddy, who had not attended the disastrous party. Bridget and Biddy had always thought they were marooned on an island by themselves as the two youngest Kerrs. They felt disconnected from their older siblings even though Chip was only three years Bridget's senior. Bridget hoped Biddy could provide some much-needed perspective on the family situation.

"Why didn't you come to my party, Biddy?" was Bridget's opening to Biddy.

"Simple. I had to work, which gave me the perfect excuse to avoid another family fight. Did I miss anything?"

"Fight is not the word. It was awful. Pup and Cissy were just plain nasty. Mimi was okay, but she left in a huff, and the others soon followed. No one said goodbye or offered to clean up. Never again will I have any more family gatherings. I'm done."

Biddy listened and said, "So, I didn't miss a thing. I'm sick of these stupid fights over nothing. Was Gabby there?"

"No, Gabby couldn't come because her jackass of a husband wouldn't watch the kids. Just as well. Gabby gets very upset by these fights, and she has enough on her plate already."

"Agreed," said Biddy. "I wish she would show Stanley the door, but she won't. She's too insecure to go it alone. As far as the others are concerned, the less I see of them the better."

"You know what kills me? This all started because Dad has a lady friend. Can you believe that? You'd think that Dad had eloped to Las Vegas with this lady without telling anyone. It was ridiculous."

"Dad has a lady friend? I didn't know that."

"Neither did I until I called him to invite him to the party. She's the lady who owned Bernice's Braid Shop downtown. Evidently, she and Dad have known each other for years."

After a long pause, Biddy said, "How come we don't know about this lady? Why didn't Dad tell us about her?"

"Who knows, but when I talked to him, he was very casual about the whole thing. But I'm dying to know all about her."

"I've got it. Why don't we just ask Mrs. Salina? She knows everything that goes on, especially in our family."

Biddy and Bridy shared a laugh.

Bridget said, "Who'll ask her? I know. Chip knows her better than the rest of us. We just need to ask him. He'll do it. You'll have to ask him because right now I'm only talking to you and Gabby. The others are off my list."

Biddy giggled. "I like to play detective when someone else does the dirty work. I'll call Chip."

Biddy convinced a reluctant Chip to call on Mrs. Salina. "Make it look like you just dropped in for a chat," Biddy cautioned Chip. "She likes when you visit."

* * * * * *

Chip loved visiting Mrs. Salina. She was his confidante and friend, and he valued her advice and loved her company. The following Saturday afternoon, Chip strolled down the street to the Salinas.

"AAAYYY. Why you here? Anything wrong?"

"No, everything's fine. I was out for a walk and decided to stop and see you."

Mrs. Salina narrowed her eyes at Chip as she spread open the door and waved him in. Chip made himself comfortable at the kitchen table as his neighbor made coffee and put a plate of cannoli in front of him. Chip's eyes roamed over the room, and his mind wandered to the time of Champ's disappearance and his mother's illness. Mrs. Salina provided comfort and support during those difficult days. Chip bit a cannoli in half and sipped coffee. "Have you seen my father lately?"

"Of course I see him. He lives right across the street. Are you fishin'?"

"You might say that."

"Her name's Bernice Kirby, in case you don't know."

"I know her name but nothing else. Do you know her? Is she nice?"

"Stunada. Of course I know her. She ran a beauty parlor in town for years. Your mother knew her. Did you know she works for Jack Callahan at the funeral home? Bernice did your mother's hair for the wake."

Astounded, Chip blurted out, "She works at the funeral home? That's rather spooky."

"AAAYYY. You think Callahan knows how to set a lady's hair? Bernice probably likes that her customers there never complain."

"Very funny. Is Bernice nice?"

"You are fishin'. Look, Chip. Your father has a right to his own life. So, he takes Bernice out to dinner. Does he have to call all of you kids and ask if it's all right? Stunada."

"Of course he doesn't have to ask us. It's just that he never mentioned her to any of us. We're all kind of stunned."

"You remember Annie Landings? She wrote in the newspaper."

"Do you mean Ann Landers?"

"Yeah, her. You know what she would say to busybody family members? MYOB."

"I get it. Mind your own business. Maybe I should start reading her column."

"AAAYYY. Then pass it to your brother and sisters."

* * * * * *

The impending marriage of Mimi's oldest son Patrick and his longtime girlfriend, Michaela, dwarfed the Bernice mystery. The bridal shower was in less than a week, and Bridget had yet to buy a present for the bride to be. Bridget loathed showers and other all-women affairs. The mere thought of a "hen party" made her contemplate leaving the country or at least the state. Bridget had tried to invent some excuse to miss the shower, but none were plausible or realistic. She railed inwardly that men were not forced to endure such events; only women had to suffer such an inane waste of time.

Bridget really had no choice. Her attendance at family affairs was mandatory, unlike when she lived in New York and all she had to say was that she was tied up with work. But this time was different. She and Mimi had hardly spoken a civil word since the hellish get-together Bridget hosted. To miss the shower would risk a lifelong quarrel with her oldest sister, something Bridget would do anything to avoid.

The day came, and Bridget donned her best dressy casual outfit and drove to Michaela's mother's home. Mimi greeted Bridget cordially and introduced her to the hostess. Bridget's first thought when she saw Mimi was that she was overdressed for a shower in a sleek black cocktail dress. None of the other sisters were there, and Bridget cursed herself for being early. To her immense relief, wine was served, and she poured herself a generous glass. The only other guests present were relatives of the bride to be, none of whom Bridget knew. To avoid having to make small talk with strangers, Bridget strolled around the house and pretended to be interested in the pictures on the walls.

The first Kerr relative to arrive was Aunt Julia with Ramona. Aunt Julia's presence would either be a delightful distraction or a complete disaster, depending upon the nonagenarian's mood. Ramona eased her charge into the living room and left. Bridget had to suppress the urge to grab Ramona's arm and demand, "Take me with you."

Cissy, Gabby, and Biddy arrived ten minutes later. Each was in character. Cissy was her usual snippy self. She looked Bridget up and down and turned away. Gabby looked frazzled and nervous. She at least greeted Bridget cordially. Biddy displayed her typical I'm here, but let's get this over with as soon as possible attitude. Her greeting to Bridget was a whispered, "I hate these things."

The shower was soon in full swing. The ladies oohed and aahed as Michaela opened each gift. Bridget wondered how usually reasonably intelligent women could be reduced to the level of squealing five-year-olds at a birthday party with their vocabularies limited to sappy superlatives: lovely, splendid, gorgeous, marvelous, and wonderful. Perhaps that was the reason Bridget hated showers and all the phony ambiance that prompted women to take leave of their senses. It was unbearable.

While Michaela opened her gifts, Bridget glanced to one side of the room where she spied an older lady, well-coiffed and well dressed, erect and alert. Bridget wondered if this lady could be Bernice. After the gift opening was over, Bridget sought her sister-in-law Rosalina, to whom she said, "Do you see that older lady near the window?"

Rosalina peered. "Yes."

"Do you know who she is?"

"I don't know her except to say that she's Michaela's grandmother. Did you think she's Bernice?"

Bridget regarded Rosalina incredulously. "Can you read my mind? That's exactly what I was thinking."

"Bernice is a hot topic at my house. Chip has been in a dither ever since he found out that your father is seeing her."

Bridget took a sip of wine and smiled. "I think we're all in a dither, as you say. It's just that we never thought that Dad would be interested in any woman other than Mum."

"Does it bother you as much as it does Chip? He's afraid your father might remarry."

Elaine joined the discussion. "We're discussing Bernice," Rosalina informed her. "You must know her."

"Of course I know her. The first lady of Coltonwood knows everyone, especially businesspeople. Bernice is lovely and loaded, a good catch for any man."

Bridget silently digested this news about Bernice: lovely and loaded, hmmm, a good catch for any man. Aunt Julia's reedy voice interrupted her musing. "When will this wretched thing be over? Where's Ramona?"

The chatter in the room died. All heads turned to Aunt Julia.

"Cissy," Aunt Julia bellowed. "Take me home."

"But, Aunt Julia, you haven't eaten anything yet. Ramona will be here soon to get you," Cissy responded. Usually, Cissy was adept at soothing Aunt Julia, but the elderly lady was more cantankerous than usual. "I'm not hungry. Take me home."

The lady Bridget had studied earlier made her way through the silent throng of women and spoke to Aunt Julia. "Julia, won't you have something? I can get you a plate of whatever you want." Aunt Julia gazed at the woman with rheumy eyes.

"Who are you? Where am I?"

"I'm Eleanor Casey. We were in the women's club at the church. Don't you remember?"

"Eleanor? Did you say Eleanor?"

"Yes, I did."

Eleanor gently took Aunt Julia's emaciated left hand. "We went on several trips together."

Recognition came slowly into Aunt Julia's eyes. "Eleanor, did we go to some castle on a trip?"

"Yes, we did. It was somewhere on the North Shore. We had a lot of fun that day."

"Yes," Aunt Julia exploded. "I remember now. Sadie Saunders fell down some stone steps and had to be taken to the hospital. Served her right. The outfit she wore was most unbecoming."

Hearing people chuckle at her remark, Aunt Julia brightened. "Could someone get me a drink?" She said to no one in particular.

The hostess asked, "Would you like some water or soda, Julia?"

"Hell, no. I'll take Jack Daniels on the rocks."

Chapter 5

Bridget decided to stop the guessing games about Bernice and go straight to the top with her questions. She resolved to ask her father point blank, which she should have done when she first heard the rumors about his relationship with Bernice. Bridget asked her father out to lunch the weekend after the shower, just the two of them. She chose her father's favorite restaurant, Sunny's Cafe, which unfortunately was crowded and noisy. Ordinarily she wouldn't care about the noise, but she was concerned about her father's increasing deafness; he frequently asked people to repeat themselves or just didn't respond when spoken to. Of course, Mr. Kerr insisted his hearing was fine for someone his age. Other people needed to speak up more and stop mumbling, he would say. Bridget asked the hostess for a table in the quietest part of the dining room.

Bridget sat and ordered a glass of Chardonnay, which she sipped with growing unease. She kept watching the door but saw nothing of her father. He was a stickler for punctuality, so it was unusual for him to be more than five minutes late for anything. If he didn't show in the next few minutes, Bridget decided she would call him. She had no sooner thought of calling him than Mr. Kerr walked through the door. When she saw him, she waved, relieved that he was all right, but concerned that he was almost half an hour late.

"Hi, Dad. You had me worried."

"Oh? Why?"

"We agreed to meet at noon. It's now twenty past. You're never late. Is everything okay?"

"Oh, noon. I thought you said one. I thought I would be too early. Where's the waitress? I'd like a beer."

"Dad, I really think you should have your hearing checked. You seem to be having a lot of difficulty understanding people."

Mr. Kerr shifted in his seat. "My hearing is fine. I don't need a hearing test or a hearing aid. Not my problem if people speak too softly."

Bridget was about to object when the waitress came to take their order. After that, Mr. Kerr drank his beer moodily, constantly looking around at the other patrons, sometimes staring at the artifacts that bordered the dining room. Bridget was uncomfortably reminded of Aunt Julia, who would do the same thing in a restaurant. At times, he seemed to forget that Bridget was there.

Prior to this luncheon date, Bridget had gone over and over in her mind how she would bring up the subject of Bernice, but now sitting across from her father, she was tongue-tied, unable to find the words to frame the question. "I'm a lawyer, for God's sake. I question people all the time. What's wrong with me now? Just say it - who is

Bernice? Are you seeing her? Simple words, simple questions. Just ask. What's wrong with you?" All of this was going through her mind until her father brought her out of her reverie.

"Did you enjoy the shower?"

She had been so absorbed in her thoughts that it took Bridget a few confused seconds to realize what her father meant. She stared for a moment and then said, "It was boring as I expected. Showers are fine for everyone except the guests. Biddy and I agree on that. Mimi and Cissy love showers. I find them archaic and unnecessary."

Mr. Kerr was taken aback by Bridget's forthrightness, but said, "You'll change your mind about that when you have your own shower."

"I don't want one, but it's highly unlikely that I'll ever have to worry about that since I'm batting zero in the romance department."

"This is my chance," thought Bridget. "Ask now." But before she could speak, their food came. Mr. Kerr tucked into his pulled pork sandwich while Bridget picked at her chef's salad despite her hunger. After a few bites of his sandwich and a few swallows of beer, Mr. Kerr remarked, "That's Bernice's favorite, a chef's salad."

"What, Dad? What did you say?"

"Huh? Oh, that salad is Bernice's favorite."

"Uh, Dad. Who's Bernice?"

"You'd like her. She's very nice."

"No doubt, but who is she?"

"I need another beer. Where is the waitress when you need her? This sandwich is really good. Do you eat beef or pork? You should, you know. There was a time when people lived on meat. Now it's not healthy, according to some so-called experts. Do you remember the time your mother cooked a leg of lamb that you kids ate in record time? When I sat down, there was really nothing left. I poured the pan juices over my potatoes and ate that."

Mr. Kerr rattled on in that vein for the rest of the lunch, but never again mentioned Bernice. Bridget paid the bill, and she and her father went their separate ways. Bridget was furious with herself for missing a perfect opportunity to have her questions answered. She wondered if her father was being deliberately vague, rambling on as he did about showers and meat with only a casual mention of Bernice. Was he trying to tease her?

* * * * * *

Bridget received the invitation to Patrick and Michaela's wedding with trepidation. On the one hand, she was happy for the couple, but she would just as soon skip their wedding and wish them well in a less flamboyant fashion. However, attendance at family events in the Kerr family is mandatory; no excuse, barring an attack of scurvy or sudden death, is acceptable. Bridget also dreaded the after-party at Mimi's where the Kerrs would gather for more quality family time. By then, Bridget would be ready for a month's long vacation in Pago Pago.

But the question that overshadowed the festivities and loomed large in the minds of all the Kerr "kids" was: would Bernice arrive on the arm of Mr. Kerr? Bridget imagined how that would go in a myriad of scenarios, none of which were good. Then there remained the matter of proper attire. Almost her entire wardrobe consisted of suits or jeans, neither of which would be appropriate for the occasion. She would have to blow fifty dollars or more on a dress she likely would never wear again.

A few days later, Gabby called and asked Bridget if she would like to go shopping for the wedding. Bridget accepted, but with some hesitation; there was always something more with Gabby, and Bridget was in no mood to listen to Gabby's carping and complaining about Stanley. The sisters made a date, and Gabby offered to pick up Bridget, a gesture Bridget again thought strange since Gabby and Stanley only had one car. Her surprise was justified when Gabby showed up behind the wheel of Mr. Kerr's car.

"Hi. I thought you were Dad. Why are you driving his car?"

"I had to. The kids and I are living with Dad while Stanley and I try to work out our problems. Dad offered to take in the kids and me, and so far, it's working out."

"I see. So, Stanley won't be at the wedding?"

"I don't know about that. It will depend on whether or not we can reach an agreement about remaining married."

Bridget marveled at her ordinarily insecure, indecisive sister. This was a side of Gabby that she had never seen before, and she wondered what had brought about such bold action. Bridget was dying to know more but hesitated to question Gabby lest she appear to be prying into matters that were none of her business. She didn't want to violate Gabby's personal space, so the sisters talked of Bernice. Bridget asked if Gabby had seen Bernice around the family home. No, she hadn't. Did Dad talk about her? Did they talk on the phone? Gabby replied in the affirmative to both questions. The mystery deepened.

Much to Bridget's surprise, the sisters had a good time shopping. Both found dresses they liked that were on sale. Shopping done, they stopped for coffee and a donut. Gabby seemed in better spirits than Bridget had seen her in for a long time. Perhaps being away from Stanley was the best thing she could do for herself. Bridget admired Gabby for having the courage to reach back to find the strength to leave an unhappy marriage, however temporarily.

The wedding day loomed closer, and Bridget's anxiety ramped up with each passing day. Patrick and Michaela were no doubt nervous, but their anxiety would evanesce into joy once they became husband and wife. Bridget had no such escape except maybe getting roaring drunk at the reception, but that was not a realistic option either. At the root of Bridget's unease was her dread of being asked when she was getting married. The age-old question, she knew, was not an innocent query nor a genuine concern for her wellbeing. The well-disguised malice that prompted the question grated on her nerves, as did the inevitable follow-up regarding the ticking of the clock. Cissy in particular loved to needle Bridget about her marital status. Whereas Aunt Julia, even when she was at her most prickly, bellicose self, never baited Bridget. Her father would occasionally bring up the subject, but it was always gentle, never malicious.

Another firestorm erupted a week before the big day when Pup found out that the wedding venue, an historic nondenominational chapel, lacked handicapped access. His Honor fussed and fumed, ranted and raved, and threatened to boycott the festivities. He even went so far as to file a complaint with the Select Board of the town where the church was located. Bridget was amused when Gabby told her about Pup's outrage, which was nothing more than smoke and mirrors. His Honor never missed an opportunity to glad-hand and grandstand. If he couldn't attend the ceremony, he would certainly be at the reception.

Chapter 6

The early November day dawned chilly but sunny. Fair-weather clouds gently interrupted the clear blue sky, a favorable portent for a wedding. Bridget awoke early and took an uncharacteristic early-morning walk. The air was bracing and a delicious contrast to the warm coffee she gulped down and the raspberry Danish she munched on. But today was Patrick and Michaela's wedding day, an event that Bridget could not wait to be over.

After a long hot shower, Bridget donned her dress and matching shoes. The wedding was in a nearby town, so Bridget calculated the time she would have to leave that would ensure she didn't arrive too early or too late. She really wished she had a guy to escort her, but one didn't exist. She would have to go alone.

Although she knew of this church, a historic landmark, Bridget had never been inside. The building was spartan white, and the sun reflected off the plain glass windows. The front doors were open despite the chill. Bridget followed some strangers into the vestibule of the church. The pews were white and brown with scarlet cushions. The aisle carpet was an immaculate cranberry red that extended beyond the altar to the back wall.

Bridget looked for an usher to escort her to a seat, but there were none. She would have to seat herself. Some of the Kerr family were already seated, but Bridget chose an empty pew behind Cissy and Carl and their two sons. Cissy did not turn around or acknowledge Bridget at all. Carl gave her a brief nod over his shoulder. Chip and Rosalina slid into the pew beside her. Bridget struggled to remember the last time that she had spoken to Chip, her favorite brother.

The church filled rapidly, but there were no signs of Aunt Julia or Pup and Elaine. Two men with guitars walked down the center aisle and positioned themselves to the left of the altar. A door to the right of the altar opened, and Patrick and his best man emerged. Both were wearing black suits and black ties; their attire seemed more suited to a funeral than a wedding. The guitar players strummed their instruments as Michaela's grandparents walked to their seats. Bridget turned her head just in time to see her father, resplendent in a new gray suit with a red rose in the lapel and a stunningly beautiful woman on his left arm. Even more astounding than Bernice's beauty was the beatifically happy expression on Mr. Kerr's face. He literally glowed. Bridget glanced at Chip and saw his jaw drop and his eyes widen as Mr. Kerr and Bernice entered one of the front pews.

The bridal procession led by Mimi and Neil walked in time to what Bridget now realized was a grotesque rendition of Pachelbel's Canon in D. Shannon and Liam, Mimi's youngest children, followed and scattered rose petals behind them. Then everyone stood as Michaela, flanked by her parents, made her way slowly down the aisle. She wore an ankle-length ivory, not white, dress. A circlet of flowers replaced a veil. She carried a small bouquet of white and yellow roses.

A distinguished man in a dark suit and silver tie stood before the altar. He was singularly handsome, and Bridget wondered fleetingly if he was married. He nodded and smiled as Michaela and Patrick came before him. He addressed the congregation. "Ladies and gentlemen, Michaela and Patrick will now recite the vows that they wrote for their wedding."

Michaela read first, but her voice was low, and Bridget couldn't hear a word except for "Patrick." Her groom's voice was stronger, but it faded as he read. The couple then joined hands as one of the guitar players played a song Bridget had never heard before. After the exchange of rings, the couple kissed and danced down the aisle to a recording of "Joy to the World," as the astounded congregation absorbed the memorable beginning, "Jeremiah was a bullfrog/ Was a good friend of mine…"

The guests milled around outside the church. Many wore looks of stunned amazement at what they had just seen and heard. Bridget was no exception. If she was incredulous, how did the older people feel? Bridget expected they were totally flummoxed.

The couple was whisked away in a 40's era sedan before all the guests had left the church. No one commented on the ceremony or the radiance of the bride. Most of the guests had likely decided to abide by the maxim, "If you can't say anything good…" The ceremony was certainly unusual if not bizarre.

Bridget wondered what kind of reception could possibly follow such a wedding. "Joy to the World" kept playing in her head as she rummaged around her car for the directions to the reception, which she had obviously forgotten. She cursed softly and tried to get her bearings in an area that was unfamiliar to her. Not only was she lost, but she had forgotten the name of the venue. "How could I have been so stupid?" she berated herself. When Bridget crossed the line into another town, she pulled into the parking lot of a convenience store, pulled out her phone and called Chip. She prayed he would answer. He did. "Chip, tell me two things - what is the name of the place where the reception is and where the hell is it?"

Chip laughed at the other end. "Where are you? Boston? The place is Bloomsbury Farm. It's right off Route 20. You probably drove right by it."

Bridget backtracked and soon saw the sign for Bloomsbury Farm. As she neared the place, Bridget thought how embarrassing it would be if she were the last guest to arrive. By now, Chip had probably broadcast to all and sundry that Bridy was lost because of her inability to read road signs. Part of her wanted to turn around and go home; the other part knew that was impossible. She pulled into the gravel parking lot, which was full and so crowded that she couldn't turn around. She had to back out onto the road, where she pulled to the side and left her car. "If I get a ticket, no problem," was another irrational thought. "I'm a lawyer."

The venue was not much bigger than a cottage. There was a garden surrounded by a picket fence adjacent to the massive wooden front door, which opened into a room with a large stone fireplace. A middle-aged woman greeted Bridget and directed her to the back where the reception was being held. Bridget stepped into an enclosed English garden with tables interspersed around the flower beds. Lilies, hydrangeas, and flowering shrubs filled the space with a tropical loveliness redolent of lavender and lilac.

Most guests were clustered on one side, sipping champagne from frosted flutes. As Bridget strolled to join the crowd, Bernice turned to her, smiled, and extended a tapered hand with expertly manicured nails. "Bridget, is it or Bridy? I don't know if I'll ever learn all the family nicknames."

"Either name is fine. And you're Bernice?"

"I am Bernice, and I'm very happy to meet you finally. I kept telling your father that I wanted to meet his family, and the next thing I knew, I received an invitation to the wedding."

As Bernice spoke, Bridget studied her carefully. Everything about Bernice spoke of class and success; her hair, her face, her makeup, her dress, her posture. Here was a woman who could be at ease in any situation, who could converse intelligently with anyone. Bridget liked her immediately, and wanted to talk more, but their conversation was interrupted by His Honor, who rudely interposed himself between the two women.

"Hey, Bernice. Getting to know my little sister?"

Bridget bristled at Pup's words and tone. At least he didn't say baby sister, but his rudeness was so typical and uncalled for. Where, she wondered, does he get his nerve?

"Mr. Mayor, your sister and I were having a pleasant chat in case you were wondering. You put an abrupt end to that." Turning to Bridget, Bernice asked, "Is he always like this?"

"Oh, no," replied Bridget. "He's usually much worse." Bridget noticed her oldest brother stiffen and silently wheel himself away. By now Bernice was talking to someone else, so Bridget wandered to the table that held the cards with the seating arrangements. She would share a table with Chip and Rosalina, Biddy and Dexter, Gabby, Cissy and Carl and their two sons.

The venue really was exquisite. Waitstaff circulated with hors d'oeuvres on ornate silver platters. Bridget declined the tempting morsels to save her appetite for dinner. One of the guitarists asked people to take their seats. The tables soon filled, and the first course was served - oxtail soup. Bridget had never had oxtail soup, even when she was living the life of a sophisticate in New York. The taste was spicy but not bad. There was little chatter at the table as everyone ate the soup, and Bridget decided to just enjoy the dinner and ignore any snide or inappropriate comments from her siblings. The breadbasket was passed around as the salad was served. So far, it had been nothing but easy politeness.

"What's the main course?" Bridget asked Chip.

"No clue. Chicken, I presume."

Once the salad bowls were cleared a slight commotion at one end of the hall caught Bridget's attention. Several chefs in white coats pushed an enormous spit, upon which rested a gigantic pig. People ogled and gasped with surprise as the contraption was pushed into the middle of the room.

Aunt Julia's shrill voice rose above the muffled conversations. "A pig? They expect us to eat a pig? Is this a wedding or a cannibal convention? The very idea. This is disgusting. The head and the feet are still there. Look at the face; the eyes are still open. This is gauche and unacceptable."

Cissy leaned towards Chip. "I think you'd better calm Aunt Julia down before she's totally out of control."

"Why me? I happen to agree with her. A pig roast at a wedding? This is beyond belief."

Bridget was struck dumb. Despite her hunger, she could not bring herself to eat any part of the animal that the chefs were now slicing with giant carving knives. Baked potatoes and green beans were brought to each table along with cranberry sauce. "At least I won't starve," thought Bridget. "I can eat vegetables and cranberry sauce."

A huge platter of meat was placed in the center of the table. Most people passed on the meat except Cissy, who took several large slices. "I love ham," she kept repeating to no one in particular.

"I wonder what the dessert will be?" asked Carl. "Maybe jellied alligator paws or candied rattlesnake skins."

"Yum," echoed Chip.

Instead of dancing, the guests were treated to an exhibition no one could have anticipated. One of the guitarists played a sultry rhythm as a pair of belly dancers emerged, gliding and gently gyrating among the tables. Even Aunt Julia was speechless. The young women whirled effortlessly around the tables and then joined hands in the middle of the room. Everyone watched, spellbound. As for Bridget, she marveled at the toned bodies of the dancers and surmised that these women were in better shape than most of the guests at the wedding. Rosalina leaned in and whispered to Bridget, "I wish I had such a flat stomach."

"Same here."

All the guests burst into spontaneous applause as the women bowed and glided from the room. No sooner had they left than a man dressed like a character in a Gilbert and Sullivan operetta sprinted to the center of the room. He flourished sabers and swords; some he threw into the air, others he twirled around his body. He was deft and precise. He ended his performance by jumping over a sword with one arm behind his back and another saber between his teeth. The guests rose and gave him a thunderous ovation.

Bridget realized she had been holding her breath as she watched this amazing show. She couldn't find the words to describe how she felt. When everyone else at her table had recovered the power of speech, each exclaimed in glowing superlatives their awe and wonder.

The bride and groom then cut the cake, which was served for dessert with coffee. The couple went from table to table thanking their guests. Suddenly it was over - the most unusual but exciting wedding Bridget had ever attended.

Later, when she was home relaxing with a glass of wine, it occurred to Bridget that the outrageous happenings at the wedding had made her completely forget about Bernice. Even more incredibly, this was likely the first time in decades that the Kerr family had been together without a fight. A milestone indeed.

Chapter 7

Bridget had reached a crossroads in her life. Satisfied as she was with her profession, discontent nagged her, a feeling she couldn't quite identify or rationalize. Perhaps it was a lingering sadness that she and Chip were no longer close. She missed the camaraderie that had existed between them, a comfort level she didn't enjoy with her other siblings.

Bridget's two closest high school friends were married with families. Neither was inclined to socialize, at least not on a regular basis. When they did get together, Bridget felt like the third wheel when her friends would commiserate about their husbands and kids. At times, these two friends seemed to Bridget like visitors from another planet, so alien were their lifestyles from hers. As much as she still enjoyed their company, Bridget often felt uncomfortable with them and knew eventually the connection would fade and then evaporate forever.

Another problem that caused her constant irritation was the unwanted attention she was receiving from one of the other associates in the office. Under different circumstances, Bridget would have been flattered and interested, but this guy was a married man with a family. His advances hadn't reached the level of harassment; he was subtle and often couched his advances with an oddball and disarming sense of humor. Bridget genuinely enjoyed his quick wit, which encouraged him. If Bridget had shown annoyance, perhaps he would have backed off, but her tolerance of his antics signaled the wrong message, and matters now stood at an uncomfortable level for her, and she had no idea how to change the situation.

Many nights Bridget would lie in bed and try to devise ways to discourage this guy, but she eventually vetoed each idea as impractical or too extreme. The lead partner, Mr. Piersall, was old school. He didn't understand the severity of workplace harassment and would downplay any mention she would make about her annoying colleague, who had worked at the firm for twenty-plus years. Old Man Piersall surely would side with his longtime associate if the situation were to reach critical mass. Bridget liked her job and wanted to keep it, but the question remained: how could she get this guy to stop bothering her?

Bridget had thought about talking to the office manager, Valerie, but she hesitated for reasons unknown. Valerie knew everything that went on at the office, but she was also the soul of discretion and would never criticize a co-worker or carry tales to Old Man Piersall. Since so little escaped Valerie, she probably had noticed Ken cozying up to Bridget but was waiting for Bridget to approach her. Bridget considered Valerie a friend, but how solid was the bond between them?

This was an unusual quandary for Bridget because her family and friends often turned to her for advice and solace, and she advised them as best she could. The role of underdog was new to Bridget, and she sweated under the combined fires of uncertainty and humiliation.

Despite the problems with Ken, Bridget enjoyed her job and the challenges it offered every day. She had just about made up her mind to speak to Valerie, but only if the unwanted advances continued. Otherwise, she would let sleeping dogs lie. One morning in early February, Ken poked his head into her office.

"Hey, Bridget. I'm looking forward to working with you."

Confused, Bridget asked, "What do you mean?"

"Didn't the Old Man tell you? He's assigning a case to both of us. We finally get a chance to work together."

"No, Mr. Piersall didn't tell me. I don't have time to discuss this now. I have a closing in half an hour, and I need to get these documents together."

Ken flashed his dazzling smile her way and left his hand on the door longer than necessary so she would notice his enormous Rolex watch. As he backed away, he muttered, "Disorganized as always."

Bridget was furious, but she couldn't dwell on her anger. She had to have all the paperwork ready when the clients arrived. Yet, she kept hearing Ken's sarcastic comment and kept thinking how dapper he looked in his Armani suit with a triangle of a handkerchief in his pocket that matched his tie.

After the new homeowners left the office, Bridget made sure she closed her office door to prevent any further interruptions. Her next case involved a petty dispute between neighbors over a fence. Bridget despised such picayune cases that she considered a waste of precious time. As the junior associate, these lamebrain actions became hers by default. She copied the law from one of her books to present to the aggrieved party.

There was a light tap at her door. "I'm busy right now," she called. The door opened, and Valerie eased her body into the opening. "I'm sorry to bother you, but the client who was to meet with you about the fence called and said he and the neighbor worked it out. He doesn't need your services after all."

Bridget exhaled an exasperated sigh. "Good. It was a stupid case anyway. A complete waste of time." Valerie gave Bridget a long, appraising look, surprised by Bridget's tone of ragged irritation.

"I'm sorry, Valerie. I didn't mean to snap at you. It's not even noon, and my day has been long and frustrating. Come in and close the door. We need to chat."

Bridget gestured to a chair, and Valerie sat. The young lawyer poured out her story about the unwanted attention Ken had been paying her. Valerie listened without interruption until Bridget concluded with, "I don't know what to do about him. Any advice?"

Valerie stood. "I have to get back to my desk before I'm missed. This is a matter that needs to be discussed outside of the office. Are you free tonight?"

By day's end, Bridget was tired. She wanted nothing better than to go home, crawl under a blanket, pour a glass of wine and listen to some classic rock at earsplitting volume. Instead, she was meeting Valerie at a small, quiet restaurant downtown. A light snow had begun to fall, and the temperature hovered around the ten-degree mark. Snow scared Bridget ever since her college days when she skidded off the road and into a ditch. But she desperately needed to talk to Valerie, so her fatigue and the weather had to be put aside.

The two women sat at a window table and watched the snow fall on Main St. The scene would have been relaxing, but for the unpleasant news Bridget had to share with Valerie. Bridget decided to get right to the point.

"Valerie, what do you know about Ken? Is he a womanizer? Does he have a history of harassing women?"

Valerie looked at Bridget, shocked. "What has he done?"

"Nothing much. He's very subtle and smooth. He's been hinting that he's like to see me after work, but I've tried to ignore him. This morning, he told me we will be sharing a case. Do you know whether that's true?"

Valerie swirled the wine in her glass. "I don't know if the two of you will be sharing a case. If you do, it would be unusual. Also, if that were to happen, Old Man Piersall or one of the other partners would be involved. As far as I know, none of the partners are preparing for this. Certainly, no one has said anything to me."

"You haven't heard anything unofficial through the grapevine?"

"Nothing. As you know, I would be the first to know. I can go through Piersall's calendar and see what he has planned for the rest of the week. I can't imagine what case would require two lawyers. We're not LA Law with a lot of big-time cases. I suspect Ken is trying to create an opportunity for the two of you to get together."

"All I know is that I want him to stop. Any ideas of how I might do that?"

"That won't be easy since we work in such a small office and Piersall is living this fantasy that we're all one big happy family."

"I know. That's another thing that bothers me. If I do accuse Ken of inappropriate behavior, will Piersall believe me? And Ken would claim that I'm overreacting, that he's just trying to be helpful."

"Bingo," said Valerie. "You might want to keep a log of what he's doing with the dates and times. That would give you a little ammunition at least."

Bridget slapped her forehead. "Of course. Why didn't I think of that? I'm a lawyer. This situation has got me so unnerved I can't think straight."

"Or you could pay a hitman to rub him out quietly."

"I think not. Who would defend me at trial? Old Man Piersall?"

"You never know. He's had some pretty weird cases in his day."

Bridget tossed and turned all night with various scenarios running through her head. She kept telling herself to stop overthinking the situation; a solution would present itself. Yet, her mind kept returning to Ken and the problems he caused her.

At two a.m. Bridget got up and poured herself a glass of wine. As she sipped a heady Cabernet, she wished she had a cat to snuggle in her lap, a nice fur ball to pet and stroke.

Absent a feline, she had only herself and a half-empty glass and no new ideas or solutions.

After a few hours of fitful sleep, Bridget dragged herself out of bed, swallowed two aspirin to tame a raging headache, downed a cup of black coffee, and ate two Pop Tarts before heading for the office a nervous wreck. Valerie raised her eyebrows but said nothing when Bridget arrived for work. The day would feature two house closings and three will preparations. By legal standards, this was an easy day except for all the paperwork that needed to be prepared in advance of each meeting. But this also meant that Bridget could hole up in her office with the door closed and just set her mind to getting the work done.

The day went smoothly with all her clients satisfied. Bridget worked on a case that demanded some research and a trip to the library. She was deep into a law tome when Ken rudely interrupted her. "Mr. Piersall would like to see you in his office," Ken announced.

Annoyed, Bridget faced him. "Are you his appointments secretary now? Why didn't he tell me himself?"

Ken shrugged. "I just happened to be passing by, and he asked me to tell you about the meeting, that's all."

The two associates and the senior partner got together that afternoon. Anger, confusion, apprehension, and outrage roiled in Bridget's mind after only sleeping for a few hours. She was tired and cranky and not in the mood for any crap, especially from Ken.

The three of them sat in the austere, spartan office of W. Bradstreet Piersall, III, a shrine to his accolades and hobbies. The old man painted landscapes in his spare time, and several hung on the walls. The only window was directly behind the Old Man's enormous chair. Bridget stared at a picture of Piersall and his golf buddies that sat prominently on a sideboard crowded with photos and tankards, which the Old Man collected.

"Good afternoon to you both," intoned the senior partner. "Shall we begin?"

Before her boss could speak, Bridget blurted, "Mr. Piersall, what exactly is this meeting about? I never received any official notification, only a verbal invitation from Ken. Why are we here?"

The Old Man glanced from Bridget to Ken. "Well, Ken approached me with an idea that I'd like to incorporate into office policy regarding new employees. The gist is that each new hire be given a mentor to help that person acclimate to the office routine. Ken has graciously offered to be your mentor since you are the newest attorney in the office."

Bridget gaped at Piersall. Her jaw dropped, and anger welled up from her innermost being.

"Mr. Piersall, does this have anything to do with my gender? Would this new policy be put into effect if I were a man? It strikes me as extremely suspicious that suddenly there's a new policy for new hires considering that I've been here for five months. Need I remind you that during that time I have never asked for assistance with any of my casework? Somehow, I managed. So, my question again is, why?"

Ken blurted, "Don't be offended, honey. This is not a punitive measure at all. It's meant to help us all work more closely together."

"You are never to address me as honey ever again. Do I make myself clear? And if I'm the only person with a mentor, how does that help the rest of the staff to work together more closely?"

Ken smiled, oozing charm. "You're just the first to be offered this opportunity. Eventually, it will be extended to everyone else."

"Why me? I want to know precisely why I was chosen to be first. And who did the choosing?"

Silence. Bridget glanced from one man to the other. Piersall cleared his throat. Ken fingered a shaving scar. "Well, my dear, it was Ken's idea. He deserves the credit for suggesting it. I thought you'd be pleased."

Bridget faced him. "And if I refuse? What happens then? Do I get fired? Will I be watched and hounded every minute? This is intolerable. If you want my resignation, you can have it. I will not be a party to this thinly disguised harassment. Ken is not my boss; he's my co-worker. It's no business of his how well or badly I do my job. With all due respect, Mr. Piersall, you should be the one to monitor and assess my performance, not Ken."

Ken opened his mouth to speak, but Bridget was quicker. "You can save your breath if you're about to lecture me about collegiality and office harmony. I don't want to hear it. As far as I'm concerned, this meeting is over. Good day to you both."

"That despicable prick. Where does he get his nerve? And the Old Man agreed with him. I want to quit right now."

Valerie had shoved Bridget into a supply closet that was hardly big enough to accommodate them and a copy machine. Bridget retreated to the back wall, where her head bumped into a bottle of toner for the copier.

"I hate this place except for you," Bridget sputtered.

"Quiet. Do you want them to hear you?"

"I don't care who hears me. If I had a gun, I'd shoot every one of them."

"Calm down, Bridget. Take three deep breaths."

Bridget did.

"Feel better now?"

"Maybe. But I still can't believe what happened. How can I continue to work here with Ken constantly looking over my shoulder?"

"We're meeting after work; I just decided that," said Valerie. "You need to get this out of your system and fast."

"Ok. By then I'll have my resignation typed and signed."

"Are you serious?"

"Absolutely."

"See you at five."

Chapter 8

Bridget returned to her office and was careful not to slam the door. There were several phone messages on her desk, one of which was from Bernice: 'Call me as soon as you can,' it read.

Bridget immediately thought of her father. Something must have happened. Her heart thumped as she waited for Bernice to pick up.

"Hello?"

"Hi, Bernice. It's Bridget. Has anything happened? Is my father all right?"

"Your father is fine. I just gave him hell for not calling you to tell you about Julia."

"Did Aunt Julia die?"

"No, she didn't. She fell at home a few days ago and broke her shoulder and a couple of ribs. She's at the nursing home. I thought you should know."

"Thank you, Bernice. And thank you for giving my father hell. Does everyone else know?"

"I'm not sure if your father called any of your brothers and sisters. Maybe he did and asked them to spread the word."

"Thanks again for letting me know."

"You're welcome. Bye, now."

Bridget stared at the phone before placing it in its cradle. No one had bothered to take five minutes to call her and tell her what had happened to Aunt Julia. She had to hear the news from her father's lady friend. Bridget didn't know what to do or think. She whirled in her chair to look at the winter scene beyond her only window. Snow clung to the limbs of an ancient oak that grew beside the parking lot of Piersall, Gallarani, and Ryan. Old Man Piersall's shiny BMW sat beside the massive tree. In her mind, Bridget willed the tree to fall and crush the much too obvious object of status and wealth. She also imagined the Old Man's reaction upon seeing his beloved toy smashed into an unrecognizable heap of glass and metal. He might have a heart attack and die on the spot. Good. It would serve the old reprobate right.

Bridget put her head into her hands. Her whole life seemed to be disintegrating around her, to the point that she wished her boss would die. Get a grip, she kept telling herself. You're out of control. Do as Valerie said: three deep breaths. Okay, get to work.

The ringing phone snapped her out of her self-pitying reverie. "Bridget Kerr. Hi Mrs. Blackwell. What can I do for you?"

"I'm calling to thank you for all your help with my father's will. Everything was divided fairly and the entire family is happy. Thanks again."

"You're very welcome, Mrs. Blackwell. You can call on me anytime."

Bridget's spirits lifted after the phone call, but she winced inwardly at Mrs. Blackwell's words, "The entire family is happy." The Kerr family had once been happy too, before all the infighting that marked recent years. No one had even bothered to call her.

That night, Bridget and Valerie met for dinner for the second time in as many weeks. By the time the workday was over, Bridget had resolved most of her anger simply because she had buried herself in work. Now that she had nothing to occupy her, the anger and outrage once again bubbled to the surface.

Valerie arrived first and was seated at a corner table. She had ordered a glass of wine for herself and Bridget. After the first sip, Bridget felt a calm of sorts settle upon her. After the second sip, she became loquacious.

"I'm still furious at Ken and the Old Man, but I'm also mad at my family. My elderly aunt fell, and only my father's lady friend took the trouble to call me. Can you believe that? My father didn't bother, nor did any of my siblings. I feel like everyone is pushing me aside as inconsequential. Being degraded at work is one thing, but for my family to treat me as if I don't matter really hurts."

Valerie said nothing.

Bridget continued. "My family has been weird ever since my brother went MIA in Vietnam. We were all supporting each other when his remains were found. Then my mother got sick and died. Ever since, the family has been slowly disintegrating. It seems like they all blame me or expect me to fix everything. I can't do that, so now they've ostracized me. You're the only person I can trust and talk to."

After a short pause, Valerie spoke. "I can understand your anger at the situation at work, but aren't you being a little hard on your family? Granted, I don't know the whole story, but you can't let your anger at your work problems spill over to include your family."

"Do you think I'm overreacting?"

"Perhaps a little. No doubt someone would have called you. Don't forget each of your siblings has a life. They're all busy. One probably thought another had called you. I don't see it being much of a big deal."

"But my father's lady friend called when she found out that no one else had." Bridget managed a tiny smile. "My father is so smitten he's acting like he's sixteen again. He doesn't know if he's coming or going. It's kind of cute, but also annoying."

Valerie furrowed her brow. "Why is it annoying? Surely, you must want your father to be happy."

Before Bridget could speak, the waiter placed a steaming plate of chicken parm in front of her. Between bites, she tried to explain. "I don't really know why. He deserves to be happy. He's been through a lot with my brother and then my mother. It just seems strange that he would fall for someone other than my mother."

Valerie looked at Bridget over the rim of her wineglass. "Do you want my honest opinion? I think you're jealous. Your father has what you crave and haven't found yet. Think about it. You expect your father to be content with his lot in life, but he stepped out of the mold and has the audacity to carve out a new life for himself. I think you're inwardly angry with him for that."

Valerie voiced what Bridget had secretly feared. How like Valerie to cut to the heart of the matter and speak freely. Deep in the core of her being, Bridget knew that Valerie was right.

Chapter 9

Later that night, unable to sleep, Bridget turned over in her mind Valerie's words: 'I think you're jealous. Your father has what you crave.' Could it really be true that she, a professional woman in her thirties, could be jealous of her eighty-eight-year-old father?

She didn't harbor any conscious resentment towards Bernice. Bridget liked Bernice, herself an accomplished woman, one who had built a life for herself despite an early divorce. The relationship between Bernice and Bert Kerr was built on mutual respect and love. Bernice wasn't some floozy trying to take Mr. Kerr for all he was worth. Neither was she a home-wrecker intent upon shattering the Kerr family. In one sense, Bridget was happy for her father; on another level, she was grappling with the change in the Kerr family dynamic.

On Saturday, despite her disdain for nursing homes, which Bridget believed, as a friend once said, were 'Death's waiting room', she visited Aunt Julia. All the sad memories of her mother's time in a nursing home washed over her as she dodged people in wheelchairs who clogged the hallway. One woman screamed incessantly. A man tried to pull her onto his lap. Bridget had to suppress the urge to turn around and run out the door.

Aunt Julia was in bed. Her eyes were closed, and her breathing so shallow Bridget wondered if Aunt Julia was dead. Her pallor was strikingly white, like curdled milk. Livid purplish-yellow bruises ran the length of both arms. Her left shoulder was heavily bandaged. An IV slowly dripped pain medication into her other arm. Bridget wondered how on earth Aunt Julia could recover from this assault on her body.

Bridget settled into a chair beside the bed. She didn't want to wake Aunt Julia. She would wait, and if her aunt awoke, good. If not, she would return at another time. A nurse came in to check the IV. Bridget inquired about Aunt Julia's condition.

"Are you a family member?" the nurse asked abruptly.

"Yes. I'm her great-niece. My name is Bridget Kerr."

"So, then you know your aunt is in a medically induced coma. The surgery on her shoulder and the pain it causes made the coma necessary. She would not have been able to bear the pain otherwise."

Bridget glanced at Aunt Julia. Feisty Aunt Julia, who could face a firing squad and not blink, was now a comatose prisoner betrayed by the fragility of old age.

She asked the nurse, "How long will she be in a coma?"

"That's up to the doctor, but considering her age and her frail body, it could be quite some time."

Bridget thanked the nurse and left the room in haste. She had to talk to her father, even if it meant disrupting his plans for the day. She drove to the family home. Her father's car was in the driveway. It felt weird to ring the doorbell at the home she still considered her own, but she didn't live there anymore and felt it improper to just walk inside. No answer. She pushed the bell again. This time Gabby, with a child in her arms and another hugging her leg, opened the door.

Gabby looked exhausted. "Come in, Bridy. I'll make some coffee. I can use some."

"Where's Dad?" asked Bridget as her eyes roved over the hall and then the kitchen, so familiar yet so remote.

"Where do you think? He's out with Bernice." Gabby did her best to make coffee with one hand.

Bridy offered to hold the baby, but Madison refused to leave her mother's arms. Bridy poured the water into the coffeemaker as Gabby tried to distract Dylan, the older child, but nothing but being around his mother could hold his interest for very long. Bridy inwardly upbraided herself for not bringing a snack of some kind.

Gabby turned to Bridy and stated, "I left Stanley for good."

Bridy said nothing and waited for Gabby to elaborate, but Gabby busied herself putting out cups and spoons. "I'm sorry there isn't anything to eat. I have to rely on Dad to watch the kids so I can shop, but he's with Bernice so much he's seldom available."

"Are you comfortable with Dad's relationship with Bernice?" asked Bridy.

"Yeah. I'm happy for him, but I really need his help with the kids."

"Do they ever see their father? Does he ever take them out or whatever?"

Gabby shrugged. "I think you can guess the answer to that question. I haven't seen or heard from him since I've been here, and that's over a month. I'm wondering if he went back to New York."

Bridy looked directly at Gabby. "Did he abandon you and the kids?"

"I don't know. Stanley is so unpredictable I can't even begin to think about what he's up to."

"Look, Gabby. Why don't you divorce Stanley? He's not coming back. Then he will have to pay you alimony and child support."

Gabby winced, wilting under her sister's direct question. She averted her eyes and tried to sidestep the issue. "Did you hear about Pup?"

The abrupt turn in the conversation startled Bridget. "No. What about him?"

"He and Elaine filed for bankruptcy. The company is in the tank, and they'll probably have to sell the house."

This was too much for Bridget, and she exploded. "Nobody tells me anything. I didn't know about Aunt Julia until Bernice called me. Now you're telling me about Pup. Obviously, I've become persona non grata around here. I'm the last to know everything. That's why I'm here. I wanted to talk to Dad and find out why everyone except Bernice is ignoring me." Bridget sipped her coffee moodily.

Gabby put Madison in her highchair, but the girl wailed and cried until Gabby picked her up again. Dylan sidled up to his mother as he eyed Bridget suspiciously. Gabby tried to distract him with Fruit Loops to no avail.

He latched onto Gabby's other arm, where he squirmed and whimpered. Gabby looked suddenly exhausted.

Bridget's anger coalesced into concern if not pity for her sister. What kind of life did Gabby have? She has two kids, an absent husband, and she's dependent upon her father's charity. She can't work because she can't afford daycare. She can't live on her own for the same reason.

As if reading Bridget's mind, Gabby said, "Chip was right about Stanley, but I thought he could do no wrong and that he valued me for myself and we would build a good life together. I could not have been more wrong. He's a selfish, irresponsible person. He ignores his kids. He thinks they're a nuisance, a stumbling block to his freedom. Can you believe that? I don't know what I would have done if not for Dad. He let me move in here and said I could stay as long as I needed to. Do you think he will marry Bernice?"

Bridget wondered if Gabby's presence with two clingy kids was forcing their father to spend most of his time with Bernice. Bert Kerr raised eight children. He didn't need two more living with him at this stage of his life. Of course, Bridget kept this to herself. Instead, she said, "Dad worked six days a week and long hours, yet he was always present with us and for us. He really is a remarkable man."

After an uncomfortable silence, Gabby burst into tears. "I still love Stanley, even after all he's done. I want him back." Bridget's astonishment at this outburst left her unable to comfort her sister. Gabby was never emotional; she always presented a stoic face to her family and the world. This sudden flood of tears left her younger sister dumbfounded.

Bridy recovered enough to get Gabby a tissue and place a comforting hand on her heaving shoulders. Gabby's children stared wide-eyed at their hyperventilating mother. Neither made a sound.

When Gabby calmed down, Bridget took her hand. "Listen to me, Gabby. Take a deep breath and just listen, okay? You may still love Stanley, but you need to be realistic about him. Your focus now should be on your children. You have a big family to help you. Your kids have only you. That's it. You have to put them first. Are you following me?'

When Gabby nodded, Bridget continued. "I think it's best if you divorce Stanley. At least then he would have to help you financially. That would at least give you some options. Right now, you're stuck here and totally dependent on Dad. That needs to change. What would happen if Dad died suddenly? Do you think any of the others would take in you and two kids? Highly unlikely. I can handle the divorce for you as a pro bono case. And I will make damn sure that Stanley is held accountable and pays you. You need to move on, Gabby, but you'll never be able to do that until you're free of Stanley."

Gabby nodded but said nothing. Madison crawled into her lap, and Gabby rocked her. Dylan crept to her side and dug his face into her shoulder. The poignancy of the scene broke Bridget's heart.

From outside came the sound of a car door closing, followed closely by another. Mr. Kerr and Bernice walked into the kitchen seconds later. Bernice's smile dissolved when she saw two children clinging to their distraught mother. "What's wrong?" She asked no one in particular.

Mr. Kerr reached for Dylan, but the boy clung tenacious-ly to his mother. No one spoke until Bridget explained. "Gabby's upset about Stanley, and I tried to get her so see that she needs to divorce him and get on with her life. Naturally, she's upset by the whole situation."

"Why are you here, Bridy?" asked her father. "Did you just come for a visit, or did Gabby call you?"

Momentarily confused, Bridy muttered, "I came over for a visit, but I didn't expect to find Gabby and the kids still here." Her confidence restored, she continued, "I came to see you, Dad, to ask you why no one tells me anything that goes on. Bernice told me about Aunt Julia, and Gabby told me about Pup. I feel like I'm marooned on a desert island, totally out of touch with the world."

Mr. Kerr's eyes flashed to Bernice for help. Bernice's smile was conciliatory. "I'm afraid I'm the reason your fa-ther seems so neglectful. I've got him on the go constantly, and when he gets home, he's tired. I'm the guilty party, not him."

The patriarch of the Kerr family looked at the floor and the ceiling. He averted his eyes when he finally spoke. "I'm sorry, Bridy. I really can't say why only Bernice told you about Julia. I should have called you, I know, but I thought Chip or one of your sisters would tell you. Pup told me about his situation and asked me to keep it quiet. The same is true for Gabby. She doesn't want a lot of ques-tions about her split with Stanley. This family has enough issues for a long-running soap opera. The only time I get any peace is when I'm with Bernice. She has been a god-send to me, especially now with all this trouble."

Mr. Kerr suddenly looked very old. Bernice went to his side and took his hand. "It's all right, Bert. You have been a godsend to me also." She turned to address Bridget and Gabby. "Your father deserves a break from all the stress of raising a large family. He always, and still, gives his very best to his children. You need to understand that he needs his own space, and he deserves to enjoy life free for a while of worry about his kids and grandkids. He would never hurt or neglect his family, surely you know that. For the first time in a long time, he's now able to enjoy life, to have some fun. Please don't take that away from him."

Bridget's admiration of Bernice reached a new level. She'd make a terrific lawyer, Bridget thought.

Everyone in the room was quiet. Bernice spoke again. "How would you kids like some ice cream?"

Neither child responded, but their mother did. "I'd love some ice cream."

Chapter 10

"Hey, Bridy. It's Chip."

Bridget tensed. She told her family not to call her at work unless it was an emergency.

"What's happened? Is it Aunt Julia?"

"Hell, no. I'm calling to invite you to Easter brunch that Rosie and I are hosting. Aunt Julia's going to be there."

"What? The last time I saw Aunt Julia, she was in a coma. How can she possibly go to your house for a visit?"

"They woke her up. She's doing quite well. The only drawback is that she has to live at the nursing home now. Of course, she's up in arms about that, but she can't live alone anymore. Her view to the contrary."

"You never called me when Aunt Julia fell. No one did except Bernice. Now explain to me how that happened."

A beat or two of silence. "I thought I had called you. I meant to."

"Well, you didn't, and I'm royally pissed if you want to know the truth. Not only at you but at all the others as well. I'm not chopped liver or a potted plant. Why is it that everyone ignores me?"

More silence. "I'm waiting."

A long audible breath on the other end of the phone. "I'm really sorry, Bridy. I'd be pissed too if I were in your position. I can't speak for the others, but all I can offer is my apology. Will you accept it?"

Another silence. "Bridy?"

"Yes, I accept your apology, but how do I know this pattern won't continue? You may be sorry now, but how about next month or this summer? Will you forget all about me again? I'm serious about this, Chip. To be ignored by the others is one thing, but your inattention has been especially hurtful. Is there a reason for it? Did I do or say anything to offend you? If so, tell me. All I want to do is make things right."

A long sigh. "No, you haven't done or said anything out of line. I really don't have a reason for my inattention, as you termed it. Time goes by so quickly, and I just get caught up in my own life and tend to just go with the flow. I'm not putting this very well. I guess what I'm fumbling to say is I don't know why I didn't tell you about Aunt Julia. That's the truth, as stupid and lame as it sounds."

Somewhat mollified, Bridy said, "I believe you, Chip. What would you like me to bring to the brunch? What time should I be there?"

"Wine and noon. You might want to bring an extra bottle or two. This is a Kerr family gathering, after all. The Wild West was tame in comparison."

Bridget had no sooner hung up after her conversation with Chip when the phone rang again. It was Valerie, who, as usual, didn't mince words. "The Old Man's had a stroke," she said.

"Oh my God, is he dead?" Bridget knew she wasn't really making sense, but the shock of the news rendered her inarticulate.

Valerie continued, "His son called me about ten minutes ago. No, he's not dead, but evidently the stroke was debilitating, and he'll be out of commission for quite some time."

Bridget often found the senior partner at the firm annoying and out of touch with the modern world. Yet she also liked him; he gave her a chance when she was a fledgling fresh out of law school, and for that she would always be grateful. But what would happen at the firm without the Old Man? Would her nemesis Ken be promoted to senior partner? If so, Bridget's working days would be numbered. She would never be able to work effectively with Ken monitoring her every move.

The events of the past two days left her sleepless once again. She had confronted her father about feeling left out of the family circle then Chip called to invite her to an Easter brunch. Had Mr. Kerr spoken to Chip and the other sibs? He must have. No other scenario made any sense. Bridget remembered with painful clarity the terrible fight that had erupted the last time the "Kerr kids" had been together. Now, despite her gratitude for the invitation, Bridget dreaded another Kerr family gathering.

Later that week, Bridget received a call from Cissy. "What are you making for Easter?" her older sister asked in her typical imperious fashion.

"No one asked me to make anything," said Bridget.

"I'm making hot cross buns and quiche. I just want to make sure no one else is bringing the same things."

"No danger of duplication from me. You know perfectly well I don't like to bake."

"Well, why would you? You're not married and likely to remain single. Only married women get stuck baking and cooking for everything, and single women always get off the hook."

With an exasperated sigh, Bridget asked, "Is that all? I'm very busy at the moment."

"Fine. See you on Sunday."

Click.

Bridget was at a complete loss to understand her older sister, who was obsessed with Bridget's marital status, despite the fact it was no secret that Cissy and Carl had been having problems for years. Bridget couldn't fathom how Carl lived with such a volatile woman. The man was obviously a saint or a complete fool.

On Holy Saturday, Bridget went to church for the evening service. The dramatic Easter Vigil had always been her favorite, especially when the church was plunged into darkness and then illuminated by candles. Bridget wondered if she would see any of her siblings there. In vain, Bridget tried to remember the last time she had been in church, probably for a funeral. She would have to do something about that.

Chapter 11

Bridget awoke exceptionally eager to get the brunch. Attending church after such a long absence had touched a nerve, but she was at a loss to explain the contentment she felt. Perhaps it was because Chip and Rosalina lived in Gram's house, the place where so many childhood dinners had been. Bridget lay in bed and remembered the smell of the house on Thanksgiving, all the food and pies, the delegation of duties to even the smallest of children so they would feel a part of the preparation. The meal was superb, but so was the chatter around the table, especially when Aunt Julia was there. Pup and later Champ would sport a bruise or two after playing in the football game. One year, Pup had to be taken to the hospital with broken ribs.

After a cup of coffee and a bagel, Bridget left for Chip's, fully aware that she was two hours early. Her plan had been to help Chip and Rosalina before the onslaught of the rest of the guests. Helping beforehand would make her feel useful and make up for what she lacked as a cook and baker. She could certainly pour wine and set the table, wash dishes or stir a pot on the stove. Such was the extent of her domestic skill set.

Chip answered the door festooned in an apron that would have embarrassed a court jester. Bridget had all she could do not to laugh at the purple Easter bunny sporting a lascivious leer that covered most of Chip's body. Bridget couldn't help but think what her mother would have said if Chip ever dared to wear such a thing when she was alive.

"I see you like my apron," Chip gushed.

"Well, it's certainly different." Ridiculous is what Bridget wanted to say.

"Is there anything I can do? I want to help you and Rosalina. That's why I came early."

"We're in good shape, so there really isn't a lot for you to do."

As they walked into the kitchen, Bridget was astounded to see most of the room taken up by folding tables: one with food warmers, another with bottles of wine, tomato juice and vodka; another looked like it was meant to be a carving station, given the enormous carving knife lying on its side.

"Want some coffee?" asked Chip

Bridget didn't, but accepted anyway. "Where's Rosalina?"

"She's in the shower. We weren't expecting anyone to come so soon."

Bridget cursed herself for arriving so early. All of her nostalgic musing of the morning had evaporated in the reality of the moment. She realized that her good feelings had been merely a trip down memory lane, so to speak.

The present bore little resemblance to the past, at least as she remembered it.

"How could you and Rosalina possibly do all of this? You must have been up all night."

"No way. We do a little at a time. Once the tables are set up, we just have to decide what goes where and take care of it. We rented food warmers and the coffee urn. Now all I have to do is cook the eggs and bacon and the home fries. Cissy's bringing quiche, Gabby's bringing fruit salad, Bernice is bringing macaroni salad. The roast beef is in the oven, and the coffee is brewing. It's too early to cook."

Bridget surveyed the room. "Chip, do you enjoy doing all of this? It's so much work, and then there's the cleanup."

Chip poured a cup of coffee from the small coffee maker and sat. "I think I must have inherited Gram's genes. No one could cook and entertain like she could. Over time, I've learned that the key is preparation and pacing. I do what I can ahead and keep an eye on the clock for the rest. Bryant helped set up the table and food warmers last night. Rosalina set the table this morning. It's easy when you have a plan."

After a small silence, Bridget said, "Chip, what do you think of Bernice? Do you think she's right for Dad?"

"I do think she's right for Dad. He's nuts about her, and I think she feels the same way about him."

"Do you think they'll ever marry?"

"Maybe. Right now, they're having fun. It's cute to watch them. They're like a couple of teenagers. I'm happy for them."

Rosalina appeared and was obviously surprised to see Bridget, but her smile and demeanor were as pleasant as always. She sat with a cup of coffee and made small talk with her sister-in-law. No one would ever guess that in less than an hour twenty something people would arrive, expecting to be fed and entertained.

Chip took up his position at the stove, a high priest before his altar. He chatted as he cracked eggs and whisked them in a large bowl. Bacon sizzled on the grill. He deftly turned the strips, then poured the egg batter into an enormous skillet. Bridget watched in frank admiration. "Chip, you missed your calling. You should have been a chef."

True to form, Pup and Elaine arrived before anyone else, but their early arrival presented a problem. Pup couldn't get into the house without assistance from at least two men. Since no one else was available, Chip roused a sleeping Bryant to help with this ponderous chore. His Honor was not a small man, and the weight of the chair made the job even harder. Chip pulled the handles while Bryant lifted the foot of the chair, thus hefting Pup over the two steps and into the house. Chip was panting when the Herculean task was finished. No sooner had His Honor made his official arrival than a steady flow of guests followed in his wake. Cissy and Carl arrived with Aunt Julia, who also had to be lifted over the steps, but she was as tiny and weightless as Pup was enormous and heavy.

Bridget greeted Cissy cordially. "I promise to behave," was Cissy's greeting, accompanied by a smirk that Bridget thought akin to a shark smiling as it circled its desired prey.

The feast Chip prepared was incredible. All the guests ate heartily, whether at the dining table, on the back porch, or on the stairs. Mr. Kerr and Bernice glowed as they ate side by side.

Aunt Julia asked where Stanley was. Gabby blushed and lowered her head. Mimi explained that Gabby and Stanley had separated. "Good," rasped Aunt Julia. "I knew that guy was a lizard the first time I saw him. As usual, I was right. He reminded me of my second husband, another lizard, even though he took me on a trip to Europe. Kerr women deserve better than that."

Bernice asked, "Were you on your honeymoon when you went to Europe?"

"Yes. The trip was fun, but the marriage was miserable. He couldn't understand why I spent so much money on clothes. The nerve. He had plenty, believe me. Money that is, not clothes."

Bernice glanced at Mr. Kerr, who said, "Europe is a very romantic destination for a honeymoon. In fact, Bernice and I will go after we get married in June. To all my family, may I present the future Mrs. Kerr?"

Silence filled the room, and then there were cheers as everyone absorbed the news. His Honor raised his glass. "A toast to the lovely bride to be. I wish you every happiness."

Hugs and handshakes followed as the family congratulated the couple. Bridget needed a few minutes to assimilate the news that her father and Bernice were really going to get married. She couldn't identify the emotion she felt: was it happiness or sadness or disbelief? Or a combination of the three? Bridget wondered what her siblings felt.

Were their feelings the same as hers? Yet, she had to admit that her strongest feeling was envy. Bridget envied her father and Bernice their obvious delight in each other. When would it be her turn?

Most of the men decided a spontaneous game of touch football would be the perfect way to celebrate the engagement of Mr. Kerr and Bernice. Patrick, Mimi's son, invited his uncles and cousins to the backyard to let the games begin. All complied except Michael. Sullen and silent Michael.

"Why don't you go outside and play football with your uncles and cousins?" Cissy asked her son.

"I hate football. Leave me alone."

Embarrassed, Cissy shrugged at her siblings, who were shocked by Michael's language. "I can't do anything with him," she said, as though to explain.

Michael stood and stomped out of the room. Chip, who begged out of the football game citing a bad knee, followed Michael into the kitchen. "Michael, my man, do you want a Coke?"

Michael hissed at his uncle. "I'm not your man. Whatever that means."

Cissy exploded. "Michael, apologize to your uncle."

"He started it. Why should I apologize? Besides, I hate him and every goddamn one of you."

"Michael, stop it right now!" Cissy screamed.

Aunt Julia shouted from the corner of the room, "What that disrespectful mutt needs is a trip to the woodshed. The very idea. Such language!"

"Aunt Julia, please stay out of this," snarled Cissy, who sank into a chair and burst into tears. Just then, the Salinas came through the kitchen door as Carl grabbed Michael by the collar and attempted to drag him out of the house.

"Get your hands off me," shouted the engaged teenager. "I'll have you arrested for child abuse and Mom for neglect. You all think I'm crazy, but the real crazy one is Mom, who belongs in the insane asylum."

"I will not tolerate such language or disrespect in my house," shouted Rosalina.

"Everyone calm down," said Chip breathlessly as he tried to separate Carl and Michael. One yank of an arm and Michael was free of his father's grasp. Chip grabbed Michael's shirtfront and pulled him close. "You're lucky there are no more reform schools, young man. If there were, that's where you'd be. You owe everyone, especially your mother, an apology. If you were my son, I'd slap you senseless."

Bridget felt as if she were watching a bizarre 3D movie without the special glasses. Everything was distorted and hard to take in. The worst was that this casus belli was taking place in her grandmother's kitchen, the scene of so many happy gatherings laden with laughter and love. Having arrived amid the chaos, Mrs. Salina wordlessly placed a huge pan of tiramisu on the counter. Never had Bridget seen her neighbor at a loss for words. She thought it impossible. But no one would ever believe that Kerr family member would act the way Michael had. Pup had been the most fractious of the Kerr kids, but he was never openly disrespectful to his parents.

Chip let go of Michael, who staggered back a few steps, panting as he stared at the floor. No one spoke. Seconds passed. Finally, Mrs. Salina could remain silent no longer.

"Who wants some tiramisu?" She asked over her shoulder as she cut the dessert. She glanced at Rosalina. "Plates?"

As though coming out of a trance, Rosalina mechanically opened a cabinet and pulled out some small plates, which she handed to Mrs. Salina. Still, no one spoke. Finally, Michael, the cause of the uproar, spoke. "I'm sorry, Mom, for everything I said," he mumbled, still looking at the floor.

"You should be," croaked Aunt Julia. "If you weren't so big and I so old, I'd take you across my knee. That would be a lesson you'd never forget. Someone take me home. I have an early date with Jack tonight."

Pup roared with laughter, and everyone else visibly relaxed. He raised his glass. "Here's to Aunt Julia and Jack. Long life to both."

Cissy embraced her son, who gave her a loose hug in return.

"Here," said Salina as he handed a glass of wine to Cissy. "I think you can use this."

Cissy's hand shook as she gratefully accepted the drink.

"This is great tiramisu, Mrs. Salina," said Chip.

"AAAYYY. What you expect? Store bought? Now, you better tell Salina how good his wine is. He's jealous of my baking."

During the melee, no one noticed that Mr. Kerr and Bernice were nowhere to be found until the happy couple walked through the back door. "Where were you?" asked Chip between bites of tiramisu.

His father answered, "I wanted to spend some quiet time with my girl on the swing. "Don't worry," Mr Kerr said as he glanced at his children. "I didn't compromise Bernice. We were as good as gold. Weren't we, dear?"

"Perfect in every way," answered his future bride.

Bridget offered up a silent prayer of thanks that her father and Bernice had missed the appalling scene of a few minutes before.

Chapter 12

"Bridget, your ten o'clock appointment is here. In fact, they've been waiting for ten minutes. Are you all right?" Valerie's voice brought Bridget back to reality as she had been daydreaming again of the events of the past weekend.

"Oh, God. I'm so sorry. Please show them into the conference room. I'll be right there."

In a semi-panic, Bridget grabbed the folder for her appointment, but she had been so distracted that she hadn't finished her preparation. She would have to wing it, despite hating to do so. During the meeting, her concentration was good; she knew the right questions to ask. However, during the endless monologue of the long-winded client, she found her thoughts drifting once again, wondering how on earth Aunt Julia could have a date with Jack at the nursing home.

Bridget returned to her office, glad that she had pulled off a meeting, half prepared. Her distracted thinking was bothering her, but she didn't have a clue how to change or stop it. If this continued, she would surely lose her job. Preparation was the lifeblood of an attorney; to be otherwise was certain death. Once again, she was interrupted by a knock at the door. She looked up from her desk just as Old Man Piersall poked his head into the room.

"Mr. Piersall, I didn't know you'd returned to work."

"May I come in?"

"Certainly. Please make yourself comfortable. When did you return to work? You look wonderful."

The Old Man smiled. "I wish I felt as wonderful as I look. The doctor gave me the okay to return to light duty, so here I am."

The senior partner slowly eased himself into a chair. His deeply veined hands clutched each arm of the chair to steady himself. Bridget waited for him to speak. Was he here to fire her for her absent-minded work of late?

"Bridget," he began. "The courthouse is short of public defenders, and every firm in the area has been asked to assign one lawyer to become a public defender. Since you're the newest person in the office, I'm afraid you will have to add that to your workload."

Stunned, Bridget stammered, "I can hardly keep up with my work as it is. I can't possibly take on anything else."

"I'm sorry. I know you have your hands full, but this would only be maybe once or twice a month, if that. It shouldn't be too onerous for you."

Bridget took a few seconds to absorb what the Old Man said. "Well, I guess I don't have a choice, do I?"

"You're a quick study, Bridget. I know you'll be fine."

Bridget fumed for the rest of the day. Her anger settled on Valerie. Why hadn't Valerie told her this was coming? She knew everything that went on in the office. She hadn't even mentioned that the Old Man had returned to work. Was Valerie really the friend Bridget thought she was? Apparently not.

Bridget wished she were home with a glass of wine and a good book. But she had work to do, work that should have been completed by now. Bridget reached for one of her law school textbooks to do some research for a case. She heard Valerie's indistinct voice through the closed door. "Good night, Bridget."

"Night, Val."

Bridget holed up in her office with the ponderous text before her when the old fog of distraction overcame her. Her thoughts kept veering toward her mother. As hard as she tried to keep her mind on her reading, the insistent memory of her mother refused to be squelched. She remembered going shopping with her mother and Biddy, and how she and Biddy would have to fetch items like bread and milk. Ahh, the meals the family used to have: lamb chops, hot dogs and beans, roasted chicken, bacon and eggs on weekends, the ever-present half gallon of ice cream in the freezer. The boiled dinner of ham and potatoes, fish on Fridays, pasta with Mrs. Salina's sauce and meatballs. How Mum and Dad would have a glass of Salina's wine with the meal. Bridget remembered how hard her mother worked, and she never complained, at least not in front of the kids.

Then Champ went MIA and everything changed. Her mother became a lost soul. Some days she could function, and on other days she couldn't get out of bed. The memories were now divided in half: before and after Champ went missing.

What a wrenching pain it must be not to know if your child is alive or dead. Then Bridget's mind wandered to Cissy, and the trouble she was having with her oldest son, Michael. Cissy was anxious, a chain smoker, and a closet drinker. Had Michael made her that way or was Michael a problem because of his mother?

A knock on the door startled Bridget out of her reverie. A man from the cleaning crew poked his head inside. "You're working really late tonight, Miss Kerr, but I need to vacuum the rug."

"I'm so sorry. I lost track of the time completely. I'll be out of here in five minutes."

Bridget hastily replaced the tome she had attempted to read and packed her briefcase. On her way out, she glanced at the clock. It was seven-thirty. She spent two and a half hours daydreaming and musing about the past. Now she would have to start her day earlier than usual tomorrow to do the research that should have been done this evening.

At home, Bridget poured herself a heady glass of Chardonnay and ate a quick supper of leftovers. I hate living alone, she decided. I hate my job. I hate my life. Now she sounded like her nephew, the hapless Michael. What's missing? What's wrong with me? My father found love in his old age. Most of my sibs are happy in their relationships. Maybe I should go into analysis to discuss my feelings. For now, I'll have another glass of wine and say the hell with it all.

Bridget did not go into analysis. Instead, she returned to work and her usual routine, but she grilled Valerie about Old Man Piersall's unexpected return to the office, and the public defender bombshell. Valerie denied all knowledge of either. Although not totally disillusioned, Bridget wondered somewhat about Valerie, if she was telling the whole truth. In the end, Bridget took Valerie at her word. After all, she was Bridget's only ally at the office.

Bridget looked over her schedule of appointments and was astounded to see her father's name. Why would he make an appointment instead of contacting her directly? Her first impulse was to call him, but she had a lot of work to do to prepare for her morning clients.

Mr. Kerr showed up promptly at four. Valerie escorted him to the conference room and knocked on Bridget's door to let her know he was ready. "Dad, what do you need to discuss that we can't do privately?" was her first question. Her father took both of her hands in his and kissed the top of her forehead. "Relax, honey. It's all good."

"Dad, would you like some coffee or water before we start?"

"No, thanks. Let's get down to business."

"What's on your mind, Dad?" Bridget prodded.

Mr. Kerr cleared his throat. "I've decided to sell the house to Gabby."

Bridget took a deep breath. "What did you say? You want to sell the house to Gabby? Dad, what are you thinking? Don't you know this will start a Kerr family war?"

A pained expression creased Mr. Kerr's face, and Bridget knew she had flicked a nerve about Champ. "I'm sorry, Dad. Bad choice of words, but you know no one will be happy about this."

"Hold your horses and hear me out. As you know, Bernice and I are going to live in her house. As you also know, Bernice has no children. So, we decided to give equal shares of that house to you and your six other siblings. Gabby is not included since she will have the other house. We'd like to have this business over and done with before the wedding."

Bridget narrowed her eyes at her father. "Bernice is fine with this?"

"Absolutely. It was her idea."

"I have to ask you, Dad. What if you and Bernice divorce?"

"That won't happen. Could we sign the papers before the end of the week? I expect you'll charge what you would charge anyone else?"

"I have no choice in that matter. I have to charge you the firm's rate."

"Bernice will need to change her will. Can you do that also?"

"Of course, Dad. I am a lawyer, after all. I'll have to look at the schedule to see when the two of you can come in."

"Fine, honey. You know Aunt Julia's buying a new hat for the wedding? She says she wants to look like Queen Elizabeth."

Bridget would dutifully prepare the paperwork and set the legal proceedings into gear. That was the easy part. She deliberately avoided asking her father the fifty-thousand-dollar question: Do the other Kerr "kids" know? If not, who would tell them? Bridget tried not to think about how each would react. *I really need a vacation from the family and the firm,* she decided.

As she worked to prepare the paperwork for the sale of the house, Pup called and exploded. "Can't you stop the sale of the house to Gabby? I planned to buy that house. I gave in when Chip wanted to buy Gram's house because I knew I could buy the family house. Now Dad has pulled the rug out from under me."

Bridget was miserably tempted to ask how Pup could buy a house when he was mired in debt, but in the interest of family harmony, she refrained. Pup continued. "Besides, who else would be interested in such an old house that needs a ton of work? I'm the only one who could manage that and come out ahead."

"Pup," Bridget said with all the patience she could muster. "You know I can't talk about this to you. Dad and Bernice have hired me as their lawyer to handle the sale. That's what I intend to do, regardless of the ramifications to the family."

"So, you won't talk to me?"

"I just told you I can't discuss it. Obviously, Dad told you, which is more than he did for the rest of us. If you want to talk, call Dad and discuss it with him."

The Kerr "kids" gathered at Chip's home to discuss the upheaval that their father's decision had brought about. Bridget had been adamantly against such a meeting since these conclaves always ignited old resentments and conflicts and sparked new ones. But Pup decided they all, with the exception of Gabby, needed to meet to voice their feelings. Mimi, Cissy, Pup, Bridget and Biddy sat around the kitchen table with Chip in varying degrees of umbrage and in some cases, rage.

"What gets me," stated Cissy, "is that Dad never asked any of us what we thought. He just went ahead and decided on his own. And I wonder if Bernice is a gold digger who'll take everything Dad has and leave him flat. I don't trust her. You can bet she has something up her sleeve."

"I agree," interjected Biddy. "Why would Bernice agree to leave us her house? She really doesn't know us. It all seems fishy to me."

Chip raised his arms in a conciliatory gesture. "Now, hold on, everybody. Let's try to be rational about this. I think it's really nice that Bernice wants to leave her house to us. Most people wouldn't even consider doing such a thing. The way I see it is we all benefit from Bernice's generosity."

"You would think that, Chip. You're so naïve," said Cissy. "I think Bernice will take Dad for a ride, divorce him, and then Dad and all of us, except Gabby, will end up getting screwed."

Bridget could remain silent no longer. "Cissy, why are you always so negative? No matter what the issue, you see nothing but unavoidable disaster. You and your attitude really irk me."

Cissy shot back, "You're probably in cahoots with Bernice. That's why she and Dad had you do all this legal work. Will you be getting a bigger cut than the rest of us? I don't trust any lawyer, even one who happens to be my sister."

Now the table was in an uproar. Everyone except for Chip and Bridget was yelling and pointing fingers. "Stop this right now!" Chip yelled. "I will not have such behavior in my home. Either you all calm down or get the hell out."

Mimi took him literally. She rose and addressed her siblings. "I refuse to listen to any more of this nonsense. What would Dad think? Or Mum? This is disgusting that our family has disintegrated into a bunch of bellowing yahoos. Pup and Cissy, you should be ashamed of yourselves. I'm glad my kids aren't here. I wouldn't want them to see the level some of their uncles and aunts have sunk to. Some of you are exactly what I don't want my kids to be." Mimi grabbed her purse and flung herself out the door.

"What the hell's wrong with her?" asked Pup. "Obviously, her kids are little angels, and she doesn't want any trouble in paradise. Where were we?"

The tumult subsided as Mimi's words seemed to strike a chord with her siblings, save for His Honor who evidently had a flashback to his tenure as mayor when he said, "Who wants to speak next? You have the floor." No one obliged him. "Come on, is everyone going to roll over and play dead just because Mimi is in a snit? Who cares what she thinks? She's an ass anyway."

Finally, Bridget spoke. "In the final analysis, Dad has done what he thought was in the best interest of each of us. I believe Bernice has acted in good faith as well."

"Why is Gabby so special that Dad sold the house to her?" Biddy raised her chin at Bridget like a defiant child baiting a parent. "Dexter and I don't own a house, but we were never considered. Dad just decided that Gabby would have it. End of discussion, as Dad would say."

Chip patiently explained, "Biddy, Gabby has two small children and no husband. Her life has not been easy. Why begrudge her the sale of the house?"

"It's not my fault that she married a jackass. Everyone tried to talk sense into her, but she didn't listen. She made her bed. Let her lie in it."

"Biddy, you're as unreasonable as Cissy and…"

Cissy flared. "I am not unreasonable. I speak my mind. What's wrong with that?"

"There's nothing wrong with speaking your mind. However, you should tone down the negativity and personal remarks. How would you like it if Gabby said such things about you?"

"She wouldn't dare," hissed Cissy defiantly. "Besides, she's such a mouse she doesn't even know her own mind."

Chip rose from his chair. "Enough of this. All of you, go home. I'll see you at the wedding."

Pup snorted. "I'm only going to the wedding because Elaine is making me. I'd prefer to stay home and watch TV."

"Pup, don't forget that you used to be the mayor. Think of the wedding as a campaign event. All those potential votes," sneered Cissy as she made her way out the door. "I can't think of anything that would make me enjoy it."

Chapter 13

"It's never been this bad," Bridget confided to Valerie over a shared plate of ribs a few nights after the family debacle. "I don't think I know my family anymore. Except for Mimi and Chip, they're all a bunch of backbiters and whiners. Of course, I expected pushback, but not the hostility that they showed the other night. If I could divorce my family, I would."

Valerie listened in silence, which irked Bridget. She had been hoping the Valerie would help her find a solution or at least offer solace, but Valerie merely provided a listening ear. When Valerie spoke, Bridget found her words more annoying than her silence.

"Bridget," she began. "I'm no expert on family dynamics, but I think you're overreacting. You come from a big family, and each member has their own personality and way of thinking. Okay, some are negative and a pain in the butt, but you need to accept them as they are, not as you wish them to be. You can't change them, so you have to meet them where they are. This will blow over like all the other family fights you've told me about. Stewing over it only hurts you, not them."

Bridget absorbed this in silence. She knew Valerie was right, and the truth rankled like a persistent toothache.

"Thank you for your candor and your honesty," Bridget finally said. "I'm sorry to constantly burden you with my family issues, but frankly, you are the only person I can talk to. I really appreciate your patience. Do you think I need to see a shrink? I don't know how to distance myself from my family problems."

Valerie studied her wine glass as Bridget spoke, then looked up with fierce determination in her eyes. "No. I don't think you need to see a shrink. What you need is someone or something in your life to concentrate on. Only then will you be able to put your family problems into perspective. Right now, you're a one-trick pony, so you take the family fights much too seriously. You're a smart woman. You can figure this out and really need to. Life is too short to constantly agonize over your siblings. You owe it to yourself to move on."

* * * * * *

Mr. Kerr and Bernice married in a civil ceremony the last weekend of June with the entire Kerr clan in attendance. Pup suddenly declared his eagerness to be there after his father asked him and Chip to be his best men. His Honor could never resist being in front of an audience, no matter how small. The only discordant note of the day occurred when Cissy showed up with her two sons but not her husband. When Bridget inquired as to Carl's absence, Cissy replied, "He's not feeling well, so he opted to stay home."

Michael, her oldest son, snorted at his mother's remark and mumbled, "Yeah, right."

Bridget thought it best not to pry and let the matter drop.

Later, Bridget tentatively approached Michael, who sat alone eating. "Do you mind if I sit, Michael?" Her nephew gestured to the chair wordlessly. Bridget ate a little and then addressed Michael. "How's everything going? Are you enjoying the wedding?"

The boy shrugged and swallowed. "It's okay. My life sucks, but that's nothing new."

Bridget saw her chance. "Why do you say that?"

Michael turned and looked her in the face. "Did you really believe my mother when she said my father's sick? He's not sick. She kicked him out of the house after they had a big argument about me. They both think I'm hopeless, but at least my father is willing to give me a chance. My mother wants to send me to military school to straighten me out. As if I'd go."

"Why does your mother want to do that?"

Michael wiped his mouth with a napkin. "She can't accept me as I am. She wants me to be like Matty, always upbeat and happy. She can't understand why I don't go out with friends, and that's because I don't have any. I'm a loner. Always have been. I'm happy when I'm alone so I can listen to music or read a book. I don't need other people, which is why I hate school. I can't wait to graduate and move out of the house. My father's decent, but my mother is a pain in the ass. I wish she'd leave, and my father would stay."

With that, Michael went silent. Bridget's appetite was gone, stolen by her nephew's revelations. She wasn't really surprised that Carl and Cissy had parted ways. The real surprise was that it took so long. Bridget was well aware that Michael was troubled, but she hadn't known the extent until he finally opened up. Bridget needed time to digest all that Michael had told her, which meant she was obligated to keep all that she knew to herself. She wished she had never asked.

Mr. and Mrs. Kerr left for their three-week European honeymoon, happily unaware of the latest family issue. The day ended with an inebriated Cissy screaming at her oldest son, accusing him of causing all her problems. Michael stalked out of the house as Chip restrained a flailing Cissy. Mimi apologized to Bernice's family, but her sister's behavior clearly crushed and embarrassed her. Pup tried to offer drinks to everyone, but people shook their heads and said their goodbyes.

"I really need a reprieve," a dejected Bridget commented to Valerie at the office the Monday after the wedding.

"So do I," Valerie shot back.

Valerie let out an exasperated sigh. "How many times do I have to tell you, Bridget? You can't solve all the problems your family has. It's impossible. Each person or family has to deal with their own issues. In some cases, such as this one, it's really none of your business. Your sister and her husband have to work out their own marital problems. Same with your nephew. His parents have to decide how to help him, not you. I know your heart is in the right place. I also know that you are concerned about your family. But there comes a time when you have to back off and let those people deal with their own problems."

Bridget said nothing. She finished what she was copying and left Valerie to return to her office, defeated and miserable. Valerie had been her confidante and friend, but even she was tired of hearing about the Kerr family soap opera. Bridget decided she would remain cordial to Valerie, but never again would she ask her for advice or look for solace from her. Bridget would have to carry this burden alone, a task she simply was not ready for.

* * * * * *

Bridget felt as though she had hit rock bottom. One night when she was working at home, the light dawned. She would start skating again. As a child, she had been the best skater in the family after Champ. How well she remembered honing her skill at the Salina's homemade pond, where she would sometimes skate for hours at a time. Bridget felt a warm glow when she thought about the Christmas Eve party at the Salinas, that always began with skating before the big meal of seven fish. The house would be packed to the rafters with people laughing, singing Christmas songs, and eating the best food on earth. She even had her first taste of wine at one of the gatherings. Skating had helped her deal with Champ's disappearance and subsequent death, so skating should help her now with the family problems that seemed beyond solution.

Bridget preferred to skate outside, but since it was still the heart of summer, the local rink would have to do. She got up an hour early to be at the rink to skate for forty-five minutes, then headed home to shower and get ready for work. The rink was almost deserted at that early hour, which suited her just fine. She did not go to socialize, but rather to relish the experience and let herself be free of her troubles, if only for a short time. Skating made her think of her neighbor, Mrs. Salina and Bridget vowed to get in touch with the witty Italian lady who was like family to the Kerrs.

Incredibly, Cissy hired Bridget to handle her divorce proceedings. Cissy didn't even ask for a family discount; she only inquired about the firm's budget plans. Bridget accepted the job even though she was tired of providing legal counsel to the Kerr family. To Bridget's way of thinking, her involvement with the sale of the house and now Cissy's divorce fueled her depression and constant brooding about the family. Yet, she felt obligated to help whenever a family member asked. This, Bridget decided, would be the last time she would take on a case involving a Kerr.

Bridget was hard at work on another case when His Honor called. "Hey, Bridy."

"Hi, Pup. Is this important? I'm really very busy."

"Would I call if it wasn't important? You seriously underestimate me, Bridy. I called to tell you that Carl called me to tell me that Cissy has really gone off the deep end."

"What do you mean? Define 'the deep end.'"

"She and Michael had a big fight, and she threw all his clothes into the backyard. He called his father because she wouldn't let him back into the house. Sounds like child abuse to me."

"Pup, I don't know why you're telling me this, but you should know that I cannot discuss Cissy or her behavior with you or anyone else."

"I thought you should know that your client is certifiably insane. You might want to alter your strategy before you go into the courtroom."

"I hate to break up this fascinating conversation, but I really have to get back to work."

"Fine, but don't say I didn't warn you."

What Pup told her did not really surprise Bridget. She had been worried about Cissy's worsening outbursts and drinking. No doubt Carl shared her history with his lawyer, and it would become an issue in the divorce. Legally, Cissy's deportment would complicate Bridget's defense, but personally, Bridget realized that the judge would be alarmed by Cissy's bad behavior and award Carl custody of the boys, which would be a blessing in disguise. Cissy was unfit as a parent, and the boys deserved better. How could Bridget morally argue otherwise? Yet, Cissy was her sister and her client. It was her duty to defend Cissy to the best of her ability. Never before was Bridget so sorry that she had chosen law as a career.

Chapter 14

"AAAYYY. About time you come to visit. I never see any Kerrs anymore. Are you here with bad news or just to visit?"

Bridget felt reassured as soon as she heard Mrs. Salina's voice and her customary salute. She made her way to the kitchen, which remained unchanged: the kitchen table with the plastic tablecloth adorned with little teakettles, the stove with food stains baked into the top. The old wall clock shaped like a cat swung its tail with each passing minute. The smell of biscotti and pasta sauce that permeated the house made Bridget feel welcome but also a little sad. It was to Mrs. Salina she would turn when she needed to talk, and her own mother was barely functioning after Champ's disappearance. Now Bridget looked again to her elderly neighbor for help and solace.

Bridget sipped coffee and took a generous bite of biscotti. Mrs. Salina settled herself and waited for Bridget to speak. "I need your help in understanding my family, especially Cissy. You probably know them better than I do. Sometimes I feel like the village idiot when I'm dealing with them. Everyone seems to think that because I'm a lawyer I have all the answers. Needless to say, I don't."

Mrs. Salina nodded, took a sip of coffee, but remained silent. Bridget wondered why her ordinarily talkative neighbor had nothing to say. Mrs. Salina looked at Bridget appraisingly. "You look more and more like your mother, bless her soul. Do you like Bernice?"

"I do like Bernice very much. She's a great lady. She and Dad seem very happy."

"AAAYYY. Bernice saved your father."

"What do you mean?"

"She showed him it was all right for him to be happy. He wasn't able to do that himself. I say you need to do the same thing."

Bridget furrowed her brow. "Me?"

"Yes, you. Listen. All the problems you have are the same as your father's. When he was alone, he learned to live with the problems, which took a toll on him. Bernice helped him figure out which problems he could let go of and live his life again. You need to do the same thing."

"But I don't have anyone in my life. I know I should be married with a family like my high school friends. They don't have time for me anymore. Valerie, my friend at work, is tired of listening to me. All she says is let it go. Are you telling me the same thing?"

"Yes. You do need to let it all go. You don't have to be the family counselor at the expense of your own life. They have to learn to solve their own problems on their own. There's no other way."

Bridget felt frustrated by her neighbor's advice. Mrs. Salina was Valerie in different clothes.

Then Mrs. Salina reached into her pocket and withdrew a rosary. "Do you know what this is?"

"Of course. It's a rosary. Mum used to wander around with hers after Champ went missing. Lots of good it did her."

"AAAYYY. Life isn't an amusement park. We don't always get what we want. You forget that I raised three stunadas, my daughters. My son is a stranger to his father and me. I used to blame myself until I realized they made their own choices, and I can't change them. Praying the rosary helped me to see this and to let go. That is very hard for a mother to do, but I had to. Otherwise, I'd be crazy."

Bridget left Mrs. Salina's more discouraged than ever. Had she expected her neighbor to give her a solution on a silver platter? It was no coincidence, Bridget realized, that Mrs. Salina and Valerie had told her the same thing: she had to let go and get on with her life. Yet the problem remained: how?

The next morning at the office, Valerie pulled Bridget into the workroom and closed the door. 'Here we go,' thought Bridget. 'Valerie is about to give me another lecture.' However, Valerie whispered, "Ken got fired this morning."

Bridget gaped at her friend. "Why? What did he do?"

With a wicked grin, Valerie explained. "He's been making remarks about the Old Man and how he's taking his time dying, or words to that effect. Naturally, the Old Man found out and called Ken into the office and promptly fired him for insubordination. Just like that, Ken's gone.

I keep thinking of the old expression, give a fool some rope and eventually he'll hang himself."

"Wow! I never thought anything like this could happen. Not that I'm sad that Ken is gone. He's a creep. You just made my day."

Elated, Bridget returned to her office and closed the door. She didn't know what made her happier — what happened to her old nemesis, Ken, or the fact that she was back in Valerie's good graces. Valerie had hardly spoken to Bridget since that ill-fated dinner, and Bridget missed having a confidante. Evidently, Valerie decided to call a truce, and Bridget could not have been happier.

In the days and weeks that followed Ken's dismissal, Bridget realized she was no longer spending her day with a clenched jaw and hunched shoulders. The tension had been almost palpable, and now that it was over, she marveled at how toxic the office had been. Valerie told her that it was the young law clerk who blew the whistle on Ken. Since the day she arrived, Ken had somehow managed to make her his personal assistant. She spent most of her time in the law library researching cases for Ken. Finally, she was so overworked she flatly told the Old Man that she could no longer shoulder such a demanding workload. That and Ken's derogatory remarks about the Old Man's health sounded the death knell for Ken.

Once Ken was out of the office, Bridget's demeanor and outlook improved considerably. She hadn't realized how much Ken's malign presence was affecting her. It seemed she was always looking over her shoulder, always wary. Now that the burden was removed, she realized how great the weight had been. Skating before work was also instrumental in helping her to relax and focus better. For the first time in a long time, Bridget looked forward to work; she no longer dreaded Sunday nights.

Bridget had always worked high-pressure jobs, and thrived on imminent deadlines and demanding bosses, but she played as hard as she worked during her time working retail in New York. She never learned the art of relaxation. Her on switch was never off. When she had a bad day, and there were many, she would soothe herself over giant highballs with her equally overworked colleagues. Such a soulless lifestyle was impossible to sustain, and she escaped the rat race after five tumultuous years.

Since her return to her hometown, Bridget's life was much more sedate. Wine in moderation replaced the highballs, and she was usually in bed before ten on weeknights. She often wondered if she was a typical type A personality, and she used her over-involvement with her family as an excuse to be always busy and always needed, the go-to person for every crisis. Why, she asked herself incessantly, did she always have to be in the thick of things? Was it a character flaw or part of her genetic makeup? In one sense, she was much akin to Pup, who had to dominate whatever the issue. As a result of his hard-charging personality, Pup owned a whole host of medical problems, with cardiovascular disease at the forefront. The former football star now spent his days wheelchair bound, the disgraced former mayor of Coltonwood.

Yet she also differed from Pup; she didn't take foolish chances or throw caution to the wind and hope for the best. Bridget was deliberate and reasonable in all that she did. She was perfectly suited to a career in law.

Chapter 15

When Bridget received notice of the court date for Cissy's divorce proceedings, she called her older sister. Cissy sounded wary and tentative on the phone. "Hi Cissy, it's Bridy. I'm calling to let you know that we have a court date on the 29th."

"What time?"

"Ten. And under no circumstances can you be late. The judge is not going to listen to any of your trite excuses for being late for everything. Do I make myself clear?"

"What if I have a real emergency?"

"That's highly unlikely. If you are not in that courtroom by 9:45, the judge will order a postponement, and then we will have to get a new date. That's the last thing I want."

"I'll be on time."

"No. You must be early. The matter before yours might end early, and if you are there, we can start early. Got that?"

"What if Carl is late?"

"Same thing. You should both be early."

"Make sure you tell him that. Also tell him that you will haul his sorry ass back into court if he doesn't pay what he owes me."

"Carl is an honorable man. He will give you your due."

"He'd better. I'm the one dealing with Michael on a daily basis, not him. It's just like him to cut and run when the going gets tough. I don't call that honorable."

"Cissy, I know the story, and I really don't have the time or the inclination to listen to you berate Carl. He's a good man, and you know it."

"You're my little sister. You should be on my side. But of course, I should be used to that. No one in the family ever listens to me or takes my side."

"Cissy, I'm your younger sister, not your little sister. I'm also your lawyer. I will get the best settlement I can from the court. I will also warn you to keep your mouth shut. Only speak if the judge speaks to you first. Do not start carping about Carl to the judge. Do you understand me? I mean this sincerely."

"Fine. I'll be there early on the 29th."

"Good. See you then."

Talking with Cissy always made Bridget want to put her head in a drawer and slam it. The woman was totally self-focused and refused to see reason. Bridget wished she were defending Carl instead.

On the morning of the court date, Bridget awoke from a fitful sleep with a punishing headache and a feeling of dread in the pit of her stomach. A searing anger pulsed through her when she thought of the day ahead. Even a hot shower did little to relax the knotted muscles in her neck and shoulders. Most of her ire centered on Cissy. Her sister was to blame for the breakup of her family and the inevitable repercussions in the extended family. Gabby, typically, had been dragging her feet in filing for divorce, so Cissy's divorce from Carl would be the first for the Kerr family, and they were all affected differently. As for herself, Bridget felt not only anger but a profound sadness, not just for Carl but especially for Michael and Matty. They were innocent victims in this drama of their mother's creating.

Bridget avoided the office and went straight to the courthouse. She made sure she was early and prepared to treat this matter like any other divorce she was part of. The sooner she could step into lawyer mode, the better. The hearing would be in Judge Altomari's courtroom, and Bridget was pleased. The judge was firm and tolerated no nonsense, but he was also fair and impartial.

Cissy arrived on time and properly dressed. So far, so good, thought Bridget. But with ten minutes to go, Carl had not shown. Cissy was fidgety, no doubt counting the minutes until she could have a cigarette. The bailiff announced, "Cecilia J. Tynan vs. Carl M. Tynan." The judge took his place at the bench and raised an eyebrow at Bridget, who gave a weary shake of the head in response. Carl was nowhere to be seen.

"Miss Kerr," said the judge. "We're ready to begin."

"I'm sorry, Your Honor, but one of the parties hasn't arrived."

The judge addressed Carl's lawyer. "Mr. Leavit, why isn't your client in the courtroom? Have you heard from him?"

"No, Your Honor, I haven't heard from him. This is highly irregular. Something must have happened to delay him."

Cissy exploded. "I knew he'd do this. Where is he? Remember all the crap you gave me about being on time? You could have saved your breath and told all that to Carl. Then maybe he'd be here."

Bridget ignored Cissy, but the judge did not. "Mrs. Tynan, you will refrain from any further outbursts in this courtroom. Otherwise, I will not hesitate to charge you with contempt."

Cissy subsided, pouting. Bridget spoke to the judge. "Your Honor, Mr. Tynan is a responsible man. I'm sure there's a good reason for his failure to appear."

The judge turned to Mr. Leavit. "Is there any way you can get in touch with your client, Mr. Leavit?"

"I could have my office call him at his home and place of employment, but that would take a few minutes."

"We can recess for ten minutes. If you cannot make contact with him, I will order a postponement. Miss Kerr, would you join me in chambers, please?"

"Yes, Your Honor."

Behind closed doors, the judge invited Bridget to sit. "Bridget, do you know of any reason why Mr. Tynan wouldn't show for this hearing?"

"None at all, Your Honor. He is a good man and a responsible man. I'm really worried that something has happened. This is not like him at all."

"If Tom Leavit isn't able to reach him, I'll declare a postponement, but it will push the case ahead three weeks. My wife and I are going to Cancun."

"That's great. I desperately need a vacation, especially after handling this case. It's worn me out completely. I apologize for my sister's behavior. She doesn't have many, if any, filters. She will say whatever is on her mind."

The judge smiled. "There's one in every family. How's your brother Dan doing?"

"You know Ch…Dan?"

"We were at St. Tom's at the same time. I used to see him a lot when he was working at the paper. Give him my best."

When the hearing resumed, there had been no word from Carl, so the judge postponed for another month.

In the corridor, Cissy was raging. "He did this on purpose. He doesn't want to pay me, so he's going to drag it out as long as he can. How dare he not show. I took the day off from work, but I'll bet he didn't. He'll say he forgot or some other lame excuse."

"Cissy, you know it's not like Carl to miss something this important. I think something has happened. He couldn't be reached at home, and he's not at work. Doesn't that strike you as unusual?"

"You don't know him like I do. This is deliberate. Can I leave now?"

No sooner had Cissy left the courthouse than Bridget's beeper went off. It was Pup. Bridget was in no mood to listen to Pup's bluster. He wanted to pump her about the divorce proceedings so he would be the first to know. Bridget decided that did not warrant an immediate call back. She would call him from the office. However, when she arrived at the office, the beeper had gone off two more times. Irritated, Bridget slammed the office door and called

His Honor, who picked up on the first ring. He sounded out of breath.

"Bridy, a cop friend of mine just called to tell me that Carl was in an accident this morning."

"Oh, God. That's why he didn't show in court. Do you know how he is?"

"My buddy said it was a very bad accident, so Carl was likely badly hurt."

"Does Cissy know?"

"I doubt it. I knew she was with you. That's why I beeped you so many times."

"Cissy was very angry when she left the courthouse. Did you try her at home?"

"I'll do that right now. I'll get right back to you."

Bridget had an appointment in twenty minutes, so it was too late to cancel, but she asked Valerie to cancel her appointments for the rest of the day.

Pup called back a minute later. "No luck. I let the phone ring about twenty times. She's definitely not at home."

"Keep trying. I have a meeting in a few minutes, but I'm leaving right after that."

"Do you have any idea where Cissy could be?"

"None. She could be on Mars for all I know."

Bridget silenced her beeper for the meeting, but there were no new calls from Pup when she checked after. When she could finally leave, Bridget went home, where she exchanged her suit and heels for jeans, a sweater and sneakers. She called Pup again. Nothing. Bridget jumped into her car, unsure of her destination. Ultimately, she drove to her father's new house, where Bernice told her that her father was at McDonald's with his coffee buddies. After briefing Bernice, Bridget headed to the hospital thinking that if she presented herself as Cissy's lawyer, she might get some information about Carl's condition. However, given her attire, that was unlikely. She sat at a red light pondering which way to turn when her beeper went off: Pup again. Bridget pulled into a parking lot and called Pup on her car phone. "I reached Cissy," he said. "She's on her way to the hospital."

"Thank God. I'll go there and see what I can find out."

The ordinarily unflappable Bridget felt waves of panic wash over her as she looked for a parking space at the hospital. She sprinted to the Emergency Department and searched frantically for Cissy. Bridget found her sister in a small room with blue plastic chairs adjacent to the X-Ray Department.

"Cissy, how's Carl?"

"He's dead."

Bridget swiftly embraced Cissy who sat as still as a statue. When she spoke, Cissy's voice was hollow. "How could this happen? What am I going to do? He's dead, Bridy. Why? Why?"

"Cissy, let's go to Dad's. You can't do anything more here."

Bridget took her sister's hand and gently tugged her out of her seat. "Come on, let's go. I'll drive you."

"My car is here."

"Never mind. Someone will get it for you."

The sisters drove in silence to their father's home. Bridget wondered what she would do if she didn't have her father, who had just arrived home as she and Cissy walked through the door. Cissy ran into her father's arms, almost knocking him over. "Dad, Dad, Carl's dead. What am I going to do? He's dead. He's dead."

An astounded Mr. Kerr glanced at Bridget for confirmation, and Bridget nodded. Cissy wailed in her father's arms despite Bernice's attempts to get her into a chair. "It was a car accident," Bridget explained. "Pup knows more than I do. Let's call him." Bernice dialed and handed the phone to Bridget. "Okay. Yeah. Okay. We're at Dad and Bernice's. Can you call everyone? Thanks. Sure, come over if you want."

Bernice asked, "Has anyone called the funeral home?"

Cissy shook her head.

"I'll call Jack Callahan," said Mr. Kerr.

When he finished talking with the undertaker, Mr. Kerr asked Cissy, "Did you call Carl's mother?"

Another negative shake of the head from Cissy. "I don't want to talk to her. She doesn't like me anyway."

"That may be, but she has a right to know about her son. I'll call her."

Bridget said, "What about the boys? They'll be getting out of school soon. Cissy, what time does the high school dismiss?"

"Two o'clock."

"I'll get Michael," offered Bridget. "Could someone else get Matty?"

"I can pick him up," said Bernice. "Let's bring both boys here."

Rather than wait until the general dismissal time, Bridget went to the school office to see if she could get Michael out of school early. The vice principal was reluctant at first to do so since Bridget was not Michael's mother but relented when Bridget told him the circumstances.

The puzzled boy was called to the office and left school with his aunt. Once they were in the car, Bridget turned to Michael and broke the news as gently as she could. Michael looked incredulous and broke out fiercely, "Now I'll be with my mother forever. I can't stand her."

"Michael, don't speak that way about your mother. She does her best for you and Matty."

"Like hell she does. She never cooks or cleans. We eat takeout all the time. She drinks after supper, and then she really gets nasty. My dad was the best, and now he's gone forever. Life sucks. I liked Uncle Stanley and Aunt Gabby divorced him. You're the only one left that I like."

A speechless Bridget drove as fast as she could to get to the home as quickly as possible. As soon as Michael entered the house, he ignored everyone and stalked into the living room where he stared into space in the recliner. Mr. Kerr asked if he would like something to eat or drink. He replied curtly, "No."

Gabby, who had arrived while Bridget was gone and had a penchant for saying the wrong thing at the wrong time, said, "I hope my kids don't turn out like that. The kid is totally rude."

Bridget waited for the explosion from Cissy, but her sister said nothing. Bernice soon entered the house hand in hand with a tearful Matty, who ignored his mother and flung himself into Chip. The dumbfounded adults gaped, and the only sound was Matty's pitiful sobs into his uncle's chest.

Chapter 16

In the weeks that followed Carl's untimely death, Bridget remained perplexed by Cissy's response to her husband's passing. After recovering from the initial shock, Cissy decided that there would only be a graveside service, no wake, no funeral. This put her at odds with her mother-in-law, who wanted a church service, but Cissy was adamant that it be kept simple, and it was. Mr. Kerr and Bernice had Cissy and the boys and Bridget over for dinner the evening of the burial, and Cissy nearly drank herself into a stupor. She rambled on about Carl and his many faults despite warnings from her father that she should not be speaking so on the same day as her husband's burial. Undeterred, Cissy raved on, oblivious to the effect of her words on her sons. At one point, Michael stood and grabbed a bottle of wine from the table. He smashed it into the refrigerator door; wine and glass shards flew onto the floor, the counters and the table. He pointed the neck of the bottle at his mother and shouted. "I wish you had died instead of Dad.

I hate you." With that, he grabbed his jacket and stormed through the door.

Cissy and Matty stayed the night since Mr. Kerr would not allow Cissy to drive. Mr. Kerr took Matty aside after his mother went to bed and tried his best to console the distraught boy whose family had disintegrated seemingly overnight. "What's going to happen now, Grampy? My dad's dead, my mother's a drunk, and my brother took off. I don't want to live with my mother anymore. Can I live here or with Uncle Chip? I'm afraid of what my mother might do. She drinks at night and yells at Michael and me for no reason. She doesn't wash our clothes or even cook. I go to my friend's house sometimes to eat, and I sleep over. His mother is really nice. She doesn't yell and break things like my mother."

Alarmed by Matty's frankness, Mr. Kerr tried to distract him. "Do you know where Michael might have gone?"

"No, he doesn't have any friends to go to. He's probably just wandering around."

"Would you like a piece of cake Grammy Bernice baked? It's chocolate. There might even be some ice cream in the freezer to put on top."

The boy's face lit up. "Yeah, I would."

After Matty went to bed, Mr. Kerr, Bernice, and Bridget sat at the kitchen table and talked. "I feel like a blind fool," said Mr. Kerr to his wife and daughter. "I had no idea Cissy had a drinking problem. Now I understand why Carl wanted the divorce, but I feel very bad for the boys. We have to do something to help them."

"I agree," Bernice concurred. "If we weren't so old, I would adopt them in a heartbeat."

Bridget listened in silence during the conversation. She was exhausted and totally flummoxed by the whole situation. Her only coherent thought was to call Valerie and tell her to clear Bridget's calendar for a few days so Bridget could get away somewhere, anywhere.

Mr. Kerr sighed. "We can't do anything unless Cissy agrees, which she never would. I wish she would get help, but I know she won't do that either. It's such a sad…" Mr. Kerr was interrupted by a soft tapping at the door. He rose to open it and saw Michael, head down, standing there. "Can I come in?"

"Of course, you can. Where have you been?"

"Nowhere. I just walked around until it got cold. I want to say I'm sorry for the way I acted. It's just that I hate when my mother drinks. I just couldn't stand it anymore. It was either grab the bottle or strangle her. She pushed me over the edge."

"Sit down, Michael," said Bernice. "Would you like some cake?"

"Yes, please."

Michael wolfed down the cake and asked for another piece. He looked at Bernice, a terrible longing in his eyes. "I don't get cake very often. It's really good."

"You'll be staying here tonight, Michael," said Mr. Kerr.

"Thanks. Grampy, could I stay here with you and Grammy Bernice? I can't live with my mother anymore. I'm afraid I'll kill her if I have to live at home."

"That's not as simple as it sounds, Michael. Your mother would have to agree to let you live here, and we both know she would never consent to that. I'm going to talk to your mother and insist she address her problem. If she refuses, we'll see what steps we can take to help you and Matty."

"Thanks, Grampy." Michael turned to leave, then pivoted and hugged his grandfather with all the force of the grief inside him. Michael sobbed in his grandfather's arms. "I miss my dad so much. Why did he have to die? My mother made life miserable for both of us, but at least we had Dad. Now he's gone. I hate my life. Grampy, you have to help me and Matty, please."

"Okay, Michael. Why don't you get to bed? Grammy Bernice and I will do all that we can to help you and Matty. But now you need to sleep. You've had a rough few days."

After Michael left the room, Mr. Kerr asked Bridget, "Bridy, what do you make of all of this?"

"Honestly, Dad, I can't even comprehend any of this. One day I was in court with Cissy thinking the whole matter would be resolved in an hour, then the next thing I knew, Carl was dead, Cissy's drinking problem is finally in the open and neither of her kids wants anything to do with her. My head is spinning. If you talk to her in the morning, maybe she'll listen. I'm going to take a few days off and go somewhere. I'll be in touch as soon as I get back."

The next day, Bridget packed an overnight bag, gassed her car and drove west to the Berkshires. She was hoping the small towns and the abundance of nature would calm her and help her think more clearly. An idea lurked in her head, but she refused to allow it into her conscious mind. She needed to acknowledge this ridiculous fallacy and make a rational decision, which she could not do at the office or even in her apartment.

Her heart had been telling her to take in Michael temporarily, to give him some stability and peace. Her head had been telling her to get real, to stop weaving fantasies that were impractical and downright absurd. One minute she would rationalize her heart's position by telling herself she owed it to her nephew to do all she could for him. The next minute, her head would rail against such a nonsensical idea. She lived in a small apartment and she often worked into the early evening and could not be there for him. She did not lead a traditional lifestyle that could provide the nurturing that Michael needed.

Bridget returned still tormented by indecision. She concluded she could do nothing because Cissy wasn't about to surrender her son without a fight. It really wasn't any of her business, Bridget decided, despite her care and concern for her nephews. Her last hope was that her father might be able to talk some sense into Cissy, if nothing else, to convince her to take better care of her kids and to address her drinking problem.

The brief vacation was a respite from Bridget's family problems, but it was not the carefree getaway she had hoped for. Haunting antique shops and eating alone in diners grew old very quickly. The change of scenery was nice, but instead of staying four days as she had intended, she only stayed for two nights. Bridget found she was anxious to return to the office now that the whole business of Cissy's and Carl's divorce had taken such a tragic turn. The sooner she could bury herself in work, the better.

A week later, the Kerr clan gathered to celebrate the patriarch's birthday. Bridget worried about this party from the time she received the invitation. She couldn't skip it, so she would have to get through it as best she could. Bernice was hosting the party, and it was to be at the home she now shared with Mr. Kerr.

The party turned out to be a lot of fun. Cissy and both of her sons were there. Each seemed as happy as their grief would allow, and the boys looked good. Michael had cut his hair and ditched his gothic look for a pair of Dockers and a button-down shirt. He was polite and cordial and Bridget wondered if he was on some kind of medication. Bridget also wondered if her father took Cissy aside after Carl's burial and told her to get help for herself and Michael. If so, how did he ever do it? Cissy seldom if ever listened to anyone's advice about anything. In her mind, she knew best and would act accordingly, usually with disastrous results. If Mr. Kerr managed to talk some sense into her, he was a miracle worker.

Bridget watched Cissy carefully to see how many drinks she would consume, and how she would act as the evening went on. Amazingly, Cissy had only one glass of wine and drank punch for the rest of the night. She seemed relaxed and calm. Surely, thought Bridget, she's on tranquilizers or something, but Cissy wasn't spacey or robotic. She laughed and actually enjoyed herself.

Chip sidled up to Bridget at one point and whispered, "Pinch me. I must be dreaming. Who is this person inhabiting Cissy's body? The change is rather spooky, don't you think?"

"It is hard to comprehend. I just hope it lasts."

After everyone had sung Happy Birthday and eaten some cake, Michael approached Bridget and spoke quietly.

"Hi, Aunt Bridy. Are you having fun? Grammy Bernice knows how to throw a party."

"It's good to see you, Michael. How are you feeling?"

"I'm feeling great even though I still miss my dad. I'm doing better in school too."

Bridget contented herself with this party small talk, but she really wanted to ask Michael what caused the change in his mother. In himself? How could such a profound transformation happen in such a short time? As happy as Bridget was for her sister and her nephew, she wondered how long this change was going to last.

Just as Bridget was prepared to say her goodbyes, Pup wheeled up beside her. "Bridy, could I talk to you for a minute?"

"Of course. What's on your mind?"

"You're not going to like this, but I have to raise your rent."

"By how much?"

"Five hundred dollars."

"What? Five hundred? ARE YOU KIDDING ME?"

"I told you that you wouldn't like it. It's a necessary move, Bridy. Money is so tight, I'm having trouble paying the insurance, taxes, and upkeep on my properties. I'm sorry, but it's going to happen."

"Your timing is impeccable, Pup. Just when I'm having a good time, Michael and Cissy are doing better, and you hit me with a two by four at Dad's birthday party. Thanks for nothing."

Aunt Julia, deaf as she was, somehow heard Bridget's remark and immediately drew the wrong conclusion. She turned her wheelchair towards Pup and screeched. "You're going to evict your unmarried sister! The very idea. You're a scoundrel and a crook."

"Aunt Julia, this is none of your business," barked His Honor. "I'll thank you not to listen to any more of this private conversation."

Aunt Julia ignored Pup and asked Bridget, "Are you all right, Bridy? Don't listen to him; he's all bluff. You can come and live with me."

By now, several people were eavesdropping while pretending to do something else. Michael stepped forward and addressed Pup. "Don't talk to my aunt like that. You're nothing but a fat-ass bully."

His Honor glared at Michael and bellowed, "You stay out of this, you little vampire. Say one more word and you're going to get a knuckle sandwich, and I won't be gentle."

The commotion was quickly broken up by Bernice and Elaine, who wheeled her husband out of the room. Bernice was furious. "Why does every gathering have to erupt into a fight? Why do you need to spoil everything? This is your father's birthday; you should all be ashamed of yourselves."

Apologies were mumbled and the party broke up soon after. Bridget followed Bernice, who stalked out of the kitchen. "Bernice, I'm so sorry. This row is owing to me. If I had kept my voice down, no one would have been any the wiser. Did my father hear any of this?"

"Fortunately, no. He was downstairs in the family room. I accept your apology. I know you did not intend to be so loud. As for your aunt and brother, I will not be so understanding."

Bridget lost no time in relating this incident to Valerie. "Can you imagine, he wants to raise my rent by five hundred dollars. Where does he get his nerve?"

"Bridget, why don't you buy a house? You have a good job, and you make a good salary. The Old Man likes you, so you have job security. I have a friend who's a realtor. I can give you her number."

"Right now I don't know what to do. I certainly don't like this, but I do like my apartment. It's perfect for me."

"Do you want to rent forever? What will you have to show for it? Just a pile of receipts, that's what. Find yourself a nice ranch and live there for a few years, then maybe buy a much bigger house. It's also about time you told your brother to pound sand."

A few months later, Bridget became the proud owner of her first home, a small ranch on the outskirts of Coltonwood. Best of all, her mortgage payment was less than she would have been paying Pup had she remained in her apartment after the rent increase. In a way, she took Valerie's advice to tell Pup to pound sand, and she felt a sense of contentment that always seemed to elude her. This little house was all hers, and she loved it.

Chapter 17

Bridget had never thought of herself as domestic in any sense of the word. She was deeply grateful to the inventor of the microwave. Her freezer was loaded with packaged meals she could easily warm up at ten at night. She had some cream for coffee, but otherwise her refrigerator was virtually empty, and her stove and oven never used. But now that she owned her own home, she was beginning to enjoy settled domesticity. She splurged on a new couch and recliner and even a dining room set. In her quiet moments, she daydreamed of having the entire Kerr clan over for dinner. However, common sense prevailed when she decided the feast would have to wait until she learned to cook.

Bridget's mood and outlook improved by the day. After her morning skating routine, she went happily to the office. She felt as though she were just beginning to live. One day, Valerie accosted Bridget as soon as she walked through the door. "The Old Man wants to see you right now," Valerie announced, and Bridget's heart sank. 'He's going to can me for screwing up on something,' she thought. 'There goes my new lease on life.'

Bridget tapped on her boss's door with a hesitantly soft knock, but the Old Man heard and bid her enter. She waited until he told her to take a seat. "Bridget, I have some news for you."

"Yes, Mr. Piersall?"

"I've decided to promote you to a junior partnership, effective immediately. You've done outstanding work in your time here, and you deserve it."

Bridget was thunderstruck. Words failed her, and Mr. Piersall spoke again.

"I presume that pleases you?"

"Ah, yes, Mr. Piersall. I just never expected a promotion so soon. Thank you. I promise to justify your faith in me. I'm sorry. I just can't believe this is happening."

Her boss smiled and extended his hand. "You have remarkable ability. I hope you stay with the firm and become a senior partner after I'm gone."

Bridget took the outstretched hand and pressed it warmly. "I hope you stay here to see me become a senior partner."

"Highly unlikely, but you never know."

Bridget tried to maintain her dignity and suppress her excitement when she told Valerie about her promotion. Valerie gave her a sardonic grin, and Bridget knew that Valerie had known all along what the Old Man had in mind.

"Why didn't you tell me?" asked Bridget.

"Simple. I wanted you to hear it from the Old Man himself. Dinner after work to celebrate?"

"Absolutely. Six at the usual place."

When Bridget returned to her office, she couldn't concentrate on anything with her mind in such a delicious whirl. She couldn't wait to tell her family. She pictured all the things she could buy for her new home with the substantial boost in salary that her new status would bring. Bridget sat in her chair and stared out the window at the leafless trees, still barely able to comprehend her good fortune. Life was good and getting better all the time. Ken was gone from the firm. She and Valerie had smoothed over their differences, and the Old Man was his usual robust self. What more could she ask for? Bridget remembered with considerable satisfaction, if not glee, the look on Pup's face when she told him she had bought a house. It was priceless.

Bridget looked forward to seeing her family during the holiday season. Chip, the comedian, quipped that Bridget should have Thanksgiving since she now had a house. Bernice offered to have everyone for dinner on one condition: no arguing or fighting. Everyone who planned to go agreed. Pup would be in Texas with Elaine's family, so his absence mitigated one huge source of trouble. Mimi and her large family had their own dinner with Neil's family, so that left only Cissy and her boys, Chip and Rosalina with Bryant and Marla, Gabby and her two kids, Biddy and Dexter, and Bridget. Bernice asked everyone to sign up to bring something. The Kerr kids were reminded of their paternal grandmother, who hosted the Thanksgivings of their childhood. Everyone who came had to contribute in some way to the dinner, either by cooking or serving or baking.

Cissy offered to make cranberry relish and a pie. Gabby declined to bake, citing the difficulty of doing so with little kids around, but decided to cook green beans. Chip, a gourmet cook, said he would cook the turkey and make the gravy. Bernice would do the mashed potatoes. That left dessert for Bridget to prepare. "Can't I just bring wine?" she whined.

If anything, Bridget was less of a baker than a cook and she couldn't boil water. Bernice offered to bake a pie so Bridget could bring whatever she felt comfortable making. In Bridget's mind, that was nothing. As she did in every crisis of her life, Bridget sought Valerie's advice. "I know nothing about baking. I've never made a cake or a pie or anything for that matter. So, what are my options?" she asked her friend.

"You could make apple crisp. That's easy, and most people love it."

"Ok. If you say so. Do you have a recipe for it?"

"Of course. You just better make sure no one makes an apple pie. That could be a potentially dangerous situation."

Bridget consulted Bernice. No one was going to make an apple pie. Cissy was baking a blueberry pie and Bernice a pumpkin pie. No conflict of interest anywhere.

The office closed early on the day before the holiday, so Bridget had the afternoon to shop and bake. With Valerie's list of ingredients in hand, Bridget went to a small family-owned market to avoid the crowds at the supermarket. She knew she'd be paying top dollar, but she didn't care. She just wanted to get what she needed and get home. Before she left the office, Bridget asked Valerie if she would be home in the afternoon. Valerie rolled her eyes and said rather testily, "Yes. Call me if you need help."

"You'd better plan on a call."

When she got home and changed into a sweatshirt and jeans, Bridget arranged all the ingredients on the kitchen table. She had a vague memory of watching her mother peel potatoes and saying to just take the skin the not potato. Bridget assumed the same principle applied to apples. She was just ready to begin when she realized she didn't have a baking pan. After a string of curses, Bridget jumped into her car and headed to a department store and found what she needed. Traffic was grid locked and the trip to the store took over an hour. Back home, she fought the urge to pour a glass of wine and got to work. Bridget set to peeling the apples and arranging them on the bottom of the pan. That completed, she reached for the brown sugar and realized she didn't own a measuring cup. Calling Valerie was not an option, so Bridget called the other person she knew she could depend upon.

"Hello, Mrs. Salina? This is Bridy."

"AAAYYY. What you need?"

The lady was positively clairvoyant. "I need to borrow a measuring cup. I'm making apple crisp, and I only have a couple of coffee cups."

"How far you get?"

"Not far at all."

"Come over here. Just pack up what you got and come over. I have everything you need."

"Aren't you baking?"

"I have my last pie in the oven. It will be ready by the time you come."

"Thank you. Thank you. I'll be there in ten minutes."

Bridget did as her former neighbor instructed and put the peeled apples into a ziplock bag. Fighting the traffic once again, she stopped to pick up some coffee for herself and Mrs. Salina. Bridget knew from experience that Mrs. Salina's coffee would keep her awake for two days straight. Thank God it's not raining, Bridget thought as she unloaded her car. Her arms full, she turned to see Mrs. Salina standing at the front door, hands on hips, waiting to help. Bridget handed her the bag and retrieved the coffee cups, already amused by the fuss Mrs. Salina would make.

"I don't know what my family would do without you, Mrs. Salina. You're always available to help, and you never ask anything in return."

"AAAYYY. What are neighbors for? What you got here?"

Bridget unpacked everything, including the apples that were already turning brown.

"I'm so embarrassed. Bernice asked me to make a dessert, and I thought this would be easy. I couldn't have been more wrong. I'm just hopeless in the kitchen."

"AAAYYY. You just need practice. Put the apples in the pan, and I'll put everything else together. Then, you just pour what I give you over the apples. Then we will sit and drink coffee that I could have made for you. No need to spend money on coffee that's not half as good as mine."

"I figured you've done enough, and I wanted to bring you something for your trouble."

"What trouble?"

Ten minutes later the apple crisp was in the oven, and Bridget and her neighbor sat at the table to talk.

"Are you going to Bernice's tomorrow?"

"Later after I have my dinner here. Bobby and a lady friend are coming along with my three stunadas and their men. My kitchen is like a restaurant, and I cook for strangers."

"Does Chip know that Bobby will be here?"

"Who knows? Bobby will be here until Saturday, then he go back. He's staying in a hotel because he will have a lady with him. The other three eat and leave. Why I do this every year I don't know."

"Next year tell them the kitchen is closed, and you come to my house. I'll know how to cook by then."

Mrs. Salina placed a warm hand over Bridget's. "You're sweet. I wish I could tell them to go someplace else. But I don't see them all that much, and if they want to come, I'll feed them."

What a bunch of ungrateful jerks, thought Bridget.

Bridget was the first to arrive on Thanksgiving Day. Maybe it was her imagination, but Bridget thought Bernice was not thrilled to see her so early. Yet her stepmother took the apple crisp and warmly thanked Bridget for making it. "I really can't take any credit. I started to make it and realized I didn't have what I needed, so I called Mrs. Salina, and I think you can guess the rest."

Bridget was about to ask what she could do when her father strolled into the room. He looked trim and fit and ten years younger than his age. Obviously, marriage was agreeing with him. "Dad, you look great. I'm so happy to see you," Bridget gushed then blushed at her asinine enthusiasm. She sounded like she hadn't seen her father in a decade. "How can I help?"

"You can assist me with putting out the cheese and crackers and arranging the wine bottles. Bernice made some hot mulled cider that she won't let me touch until everyone is here. She's such a tyrant." Mr. Kerr's tone was affectionate, and Bridget didn't miss the sly wink he gave to his wife. He was a happy man.

Aunt Julia arrived by a chair car arranged by the nursing home. Cissy and her two sons happened to pull in at the same time, and Michael took the wheelchair from the driver and pushed Aunt Julia into the house. Bernice greeted the old lady with a quick peck on the cheek and a polite, "You're looking well, Julia." Then she helped undo the scarf wrapped around Aunt Julia's neck. It took Bernice and Bridget to get Aunt Julia out of the coat that overlaid a thick sweater. Whoever got her ready at the nursing home must have thought Aunt Julia was having Thanksgiving in Antarctica.

Throughout the meal, Bridget kept her eye on Cissy, who kept raving about her sons and how well they were dealing with their father's death. Cissy's hands shook slightly when she lifted her fork or cut her meat. Bridget wondered if her older sister was on medication or suffering withdrawal from alcohol and nicotine. Cissy drank one glass of mulled cider but otherwise drank water. Matty seated himself next to Chip, and Michael next to Bridget. For most of the meal he was quiet but suddenly spoke. "Aunt Bridy. I can rake your leaves if you want me to. Matty and I raked and bagged all the leaves in our yard."

"That would be wonderful, Michael, but it's cold now."

"That's okay. I don't mind the cold when I'm working."

"I want to pay you. I understand you're saving to buy a car."

"I don't mind doing it for nothing."

"No. You deserve to be paid."

"All right. Will this Saturday be okay?"

"Perfect."

Even though most of the family was present for the dinner, Bridget felt forlorn and groped to understand the reason. Was it the realization that this would likely be Aunt Julia's last Thanksgiving? The indomitable nonagenarian hardly touched her food and spent most of the meal asleep. Was it the house? Bernice's home was much more modern than the Kerr family home or the home of their paternal grandparents, where Bridget had spent every other Thanksgiving of her life. The dining room table was too small to seat everyone, so a folding table had to be set up, which meant some people had their backs to other people. The meal was superb, and Bridget ate with great relish. She was fanatical about watching her weight, but this was the one day she ate whatever she wanted.

The Salinas came for dessert, and Mrs. Salina was kind enough not to mention that she actually made the apple crisp, not Bridget. Bernice was kind enough to remain silent on that subject as well. Salina brought two bottles of homemade wine, and those old enough enjoyed the smooth, fruity flavor. Bridget consumed two glasses but stopped when she remembered she had to drive much farther than usual to get to her new home.

The evening wound down, and everyone asked for their coats. Bridget decided to stay a little longer to get her bearings and help her father and Bernice to clean up. As

Michael was leaving, Bridget gave him a tight hug. "I'll see you on Saturday," she reminded her nephew. "But you'll have to bring your own rake. I don't own one."

Michael hugged her back and whispered, "My mother's drinking again."

Chapter 18

Bridget was disturbed by Michael's admission but not surprised. She had expected Cissy would fall off the wagon at some point and revert to her previous behavior. But Bridget knew she had absolutely no control over Cissy's actions and decided to let events unfold as they were meant to. Bridget's main preoccupation was what to get for her family for Christmas. She had long ago stopped buying for most of her nieces and nephews since the family had gotten so large. She would buy something for Gabby's kids since they were still little, but she also wanted to get something for Michael and Matty. The trick would be how to do that without the rest of the family knowing.

Her workload had increased since her promotion, and she was absorbed in a case when Valerie buzzed her phone. Bridget wanted to ignore it since she was busy, but she picked up. Valerie said, "Your brother is on line two. He says it's urgent." Bridget immediately thought of her father, so she snatched up the receiver. "Hello."

"Hey, Bridy." It was Chip. "Sorry I had to call you at work, but I figured you would want to know that Aunt Julia passed away peacefully in her sleep last night."

Despite Aunt Julia's advanced age, Bridget was actually surprised that she died. "Wow! I didn't think Aunt Julia would ever die."

"I know. She didn't look good at Thanksgiving, but I thought she would rally as she always had in the past and still be around for Christmas. She was a great lady."

"You were her favorite, Chippie. She will probably leave all her money to you."

"Don't you know? You prepared her will."

"I'm kidding. As I recall, she named all of us to receive some share of her property. I'm sorry, Chip, but I really need to get back to work. Keep me posted about the arrangements."

"Will do. Talk to you later."

Despite her best efforts to concentrate, Bridget's thoughts kept returning to Aunt Julia, the flamboyant lady who had an opinion about everything and disdain for people who dared to disagree with her. She could be loud and frequently rude, but she also held firm to her beliefs. Aunt Julia cared about excellence and insisted upon proper decorum and manners, although there were people who thought she had none. She had her standards and firmly adhered to them, regardless of what other people thought. Aunt Julia was a curious mixture of contradictions and ambiguities; she was an enigma, a puzzle even to those who knew her well.

Bridget knew no one else who had four husbands but no children, who still insisted upon wearing hats thirty years after most women had abandoned them as archaic, a lady who had no qualms about asking personal questions but jealously guarded her own privacy. Aunt Julia was one of a kind. She defied all the odds. She lived to a ripe old age despite her love of Jack Daniels or perhaps because of it. Her mind was sharp almost until the day of her death. She lived on her own longer than most of her generation lived. Aunt Julia's passing marked the end of an era for the Kerr family, and that grieved Bridget the most.

Mr. Kerr called the family together to discuss funeral arrangements. Most of the Kerr "kids" reacted to Aunt Julia's death with resignation, but Cissy was inconsolable. She was very close to Aunt Julia and shared many of her traits. The dynamic between the two baffled the rest of the family. Aunt Julia brought out the best in Cissy, but Cissy would turn around and act like Aunt Julia to everyone else. When Aunt Julia was well enough, Cissy would take her out to lunch or to shop, and the two women genuinely enjoyed each other's company. Cissy must have felt that she had lost her best friend.

Decisions had to be made about the roles each family member would play for the funeral. All agreed that no wake was necessary, that a funeral could suffice. Bridget offered to do a reading, as did Rosalina. Chip would deliver the eulogy. Chip, Neil, Dexter, Patrick, Mimi's oldest son, Michael, and Bryant would serve as pallbearers. After the service, everyone would repair to Chip and Rosalina's for a collation. Aunt Julia's burial would take place in the spring.

There was a snowstorm on the day of the funeral. Bridget got up early to shovel her driveway and clean off her car. But by the time she finished shoveling, the car was covered again, and the plow had filled in what she had cleared. Luckily for her, a kind neighbor whom she didn't know came over to help her shovel and clean off her car. By the time she showered and dressed, she was running late, and it was slow going on the roads.

Despite the storm, everyone made it to the funeral home on time. Aunt Julia lay placidly, all decked out in one of her best outfits with a large hat to match. Her wrists and neck were festooned with her jewelry. Bridget guessed that Aunt Julia must have left explicit instructions as to how she would be dressed for her going away party. No doubt, Jack Callahan allowed himself a chuckle or two when he prepared Aunt Julia's body.

The service was traditional and dignified. Chip's eulogy was perceptive and amusing. He had everyone laughing except Cissy, who sobbed quietly throughout the service. In addition to the family, the Salinas were there, as was Aunt Julia's devoted caregiver, Ramona. Old Man Piersall and Valerie attended as well. Since the burial would not be until the spring, everyone went to Chip and Rosalina's for a catered lunch. The wine and the spirits flowed freely as everyone wanted to toast Aunt Julia. Mr. Kerr was especially ebullient, calling for more refills until Bernice quietly shut him off. Aunt Julia would have loved it.

Christmas was fast approaching, and Bridget faced her usual problem of what to get for whom. The protocol for the holiday would be the usual: Chip and Rosalina would host a buffet on Christmas Eve, then Mr. Kerr and Bernice would have dinner the next day. Only Gabby and her kids, Cissy and her sons, and Bridget would be at Christmas dinner. The rest of the Kerr "kids" would be celebrating with their own families.

Bernice prepared a sumptuous meal of roast beef with all the trimmings. Bridget expected to gain at least five extra pounds by the time Christmas was over. Gifts were exchanged and since most of the nieces and nephews were not there, Bridget was able to give Michael and Matty their presents without worrying about whispers of favoritism.

Cissy clearly showed signs of depression. She was quiet and avoided eye contact as much as possible. She ate and drank little and showed no enthusiasm for anything she had been given. The boys seemed more somber also as they struggled to get through their first Christmas without their father. Gabby's kids careened around and screamed with delight at their presents. Their innocent happiness contrasted sharply with the dour mood of Cissy and the boys. When she had a chance, Bridget took Cissy aside.

"Cissy, I know this is hard for you, the first Christmas without Carl and Aunt Julia, but try to at least seem happy for the boys."

"All you think about is the boys. Did you ever stop to consider what I'm dealing with on a daily basis? I'm trying to juggle life alone with two boys and a full-time job. You don't have a care in the world, so I guess I can't expect you to understand."

"Just a minute, Cissy. Just because I'm not married with a family doesn't mean that I'm footloose and fancy free. I have a demanding job, and I have to deal with loneliness that you will never understand. Don't judge me based on what you think my life is like."

Cissy hung her head. "I'm sorry. I spoke out of turn. It's just that I'm so depressed I can't think straight. I feel like I'm on a treadmill that I can't get off. Every day is a little worse than the day before."

"Cissy, you have insurance. Find a doctor or a counselor you can speak to. You probably need some medication. You don't have to suffer in silence. Get help. If you can't do it for yourself, do it for the boys. They need you. They've lost their father. You're all they've got."

Bridget went home exhausted and deeply troubled. She doubted that Cissy would take her advice, but there was no way to force her, and Bridget would just have to accept that. She wasn't in the habit of calling Cissy just to talk, so she couldn't pick up the phone to check on her. Cissy would misunderstand, and the situation would get even worse. Bridget dreaded the next family gathering on New Year's Eve. She was tired of all this family bonding. She prayed for a blizzard.

The snow didn't come, so Bridget had to attend the bash that Pup and Elaine hosted. Even though His Honor and his wife were financially strapped, they spared no expense for this party. The food and the champagne were plentiful, as were the noisemakers. Bridget was in no mood for any of this, but she went, fully intending to leave well before midnight. She wasn't there five minutes when the host accosted her. "Are you still pissed at me for raising your rent?" was his greeting.

"Why should I be? You actually did me a favor. If you hadn't raised the rent, I never would have bought the house. It was the wake-up call I needed to get moving and get out of the rut I was in. So, thank you, Pup. Do you have a new tenant?"

"Yeah, I do. A guy who used to work for me."

"I hope he can afford the rent. It would be a shame if you had to evict him."

"Very funny. Try some of this punch. I made it myself."

"All the more reason to avoid it."

Once again Bridget focused her attention on Cissy. Her older sister was brighter than she had been on Christmas, but there was something false about it, forced. Cissy said that her doctor had given her a prescription for Valium and another prescription to help her sleep. "Have you made an appointment with a counselor?" asked Bridget. "You really need to talk this out rather than rely on pills."

"One thing at a time," replied Cissy. "I have to do this in my own time and at my own pace."

Bridget knew then that Cissy had no intention of calling a counselor.

Dick Clark's New Year's Rockin' Eve was blaring on the TV even though no one was paying much attention. Bridget made small talk with other guests, but she kept looking at the clock and decided she would leave at nine o'clock, no later. Pup's punch was pretty good, and she was about to pour herself another glass when an excited Matty grabbed her arm. "Aunt Bridy, come down and play pool with me and Michael."

Bridget laughed. "Matty, I don't know how to play pool."

"I'll teach you. We can also play ping-pong. Come on."

Bridget followed her nephew to the basement Pup had converted into an impressive game room. Most of the younger generation were here enjoying themselves away from the adults upstairs. Michael smiled when he saw her and offered her a cue and some instructions on how to use it. Clumsy as she was, Bridy took her turns trying to get the right ball into the right pocket. She usually failed, but she was having such a good time, she didn't care. She forgot about the time and reveled in being with her nephews.

Bridget then tried her hand at ping-pong. She wasn't much better at that than at pool, but she was game to try. After half an hour of flailing and diving to hit the ball, she was tired and ready to call it quits when Mimi came downstairs, a worried look on her face. "Have you seen Cissy? I was hoping she was down here. I can't find her anywhere."

"I haven't seen her for a couple of hours. I hope she isn't outside smoking."

"I looked. She's not."

The two women went upstairs in search of their sister. Bridget noticed some people had left the party, but there were still a considerable number of guests. She and Mimi wandered from room to room, but there was no sign of Cissy. Finally, they went upstairs to search the bedrooms. They found Cissy in a bedroom stretched out, one arm hanging off the side of the bed. Mimi tried to wake her, but she didn't respond. Mimi shook her, still no response. Bridget and Mimi both shook her. Nothing. Bridget noticed a half-empty glass of what appeared to be whiskey on the side table. There were also two bottles of prescription medication.

"Oh, God. She took her medication with liquor. Is she dead?"

Bridget leaned over her sister and saw that she was breathing, but shallowly.

"She's alive, but we better get her to a hospital fast. I'll tell Pup and call an ambulance."

Bridget ran downstairs, her heart thudding as she frantically looked for her brother. Instead, she found Elaine and said breathlessly, "Elaine, Cissy is passed out upstairs. She took some of her meds with alcohol and now she's unresponsive. We have to get her to the hospital ASAP."

Elaine gaped at her sister-in-law. "If that isn't just like Cissy."

Bridget thought she misheard Elaine. Didn't she understand what Bridget had just told her?

"Elaine, I need to use your phone. I have to call an ambulance."

"Is it that serious? Cissy just needs to sleep it off. She'll be fine."

"No, Elaine. She won't be fine. She needs medical attention right now."

Bridget found the phone in the kitchen and had trouble dialing 911. She had to try three times to get it right. She could hardly hear with all the revelry around her, and she had to shout in order for the dispatcher to hear her. Then she couldn't remember the number of Pup's house. "The driver will know the house," she told the dispatcher. "There are plenty of cars around."

Bridget found her father and told him the situation. He shouted over the clamor, "Listen, everybody. Cissy is having a medical emergency, and the ambulance is on its way. Try to stay calm."

The noise ended, and people looked around in bewilderment. Bridget ran outside without her coat to make sure the EMT's knew where to go. When the ambulance arrived, Bridget directed them to the upstairs bedroom. Then she raced into the house to find Michael and Matty and try to explain what happened. By then, all the younger family members were standing beside the silent adults and watched the EMT's lug the gurney upstairs. An eternity passed before the ambulance crew slowly brought the gurney down. Bridget found Michael and Matty and put her arms around them. She wanted to reassure them, but she couldn't even grasp what had happened.

Mr. Kerr and Bernice followed the ambulance to the hospital. The rest of the guests departed hurriedly, unsure of what else to do. Elaine made coffee for the people who remained, but everyone was stunned and tired.

For the adults, the question remained what to do about Michael and Matty. They couldn't go home alone without adult supervision. Suddenly, Matty ran to Chip and threw himself into his uncle's arms. "Uncle Chip, take me home with you. I'll be good. I promise."

Michael hung his head but said nothing. Then the words were out of Bridget's mouth before she even realized what she said. "Michael, do you want to go with Matty or go home with me?"

"I'll go with you, Aunt Bridy."

During the drive home, Michael suddenly spoke. "Aunt Bridy, did my mother try to kill herself?"

"We don't know Michael. I suppose it's possible, but let's not jump to conclusions before we have all the facts."

"I'll bet she did. She's sick of having Matty and me around."

"You know that's not true, Michael. I know it's late, and you're tired, and you didn't mean what you just said. We'll see what the story is in the morning."

"I'm afraid all I can offer you is the couch. It's brand new, so it should be comfortable."

"No problem. I'll be fine." Michael was asleep five minutes later.

Bridget made herself a cup of coffee and thought about the evening. She believed Cissy had indeed tried to kill herself. But why had she chosen a New Year's Eve party to do so? She could have done it so much easier in her own bed. Perhaps she wanted someone other than her sons to find her. Whatever her reasons, she left Michael and Matty in limbo. What would happen if she died? Would the two boys have to go into foster care? No. Bridget would never permit that. The Kerr clan would rally around them and make sure they were properly taken care of.

The next morning, Bridget drove Michael home so he could get some clean clothes. Then they went to Chip's for breakfast. Chip had gone to the hospital early in the morning to relieve his father and Bernice. Cissy was alive but in a medically induced coma. The doctors wanted to determine what, if any, damage had been done to her brain.

Michael and Matty took the news somberly but without emotion. Rosalina made breakfast, and everyone ate heartily. Chip asked both boys point-blank if they would like to stay with him and Bridy respectively. Both boys gave an enthusiastic thumbs up. Neither asked to see their mother. After breakfast, Bridget drove Michael to his home so he could get the rest of his clothes and whatever else he would need during his stay with her. "Tomorrow I'll go shopping and get you a bed and a bureau, so you don't have to live like a gypsy."

"What's a gypsy?"

Michael settled in, and life went on. The doctors awakened Cissy from the coma, and the news was good: she had not suffered any permanent damage and would recover fully. Cissy, to the amazement of her family, made the decision to check herself into a rehab facility out of state. She would be there for several months. Bridget took Michael to see his mother before she left. Michael asked to see his mother privately, and Bridget respected that request. When Michael came out, Bridget went in to see her sister. Cissy looked thinner but otherwise fine. "Thank you for taking care of Michael for me. I really appreciate the sacrifice you're making."

"It's not a sacrifice for me. I'm happy to do it."

"Raising a teenage boy is not easy. You'll find out soon enough."

"I'll deal with it."

"Thanks. I know he'll be in good hands."

Bridget hugged Cissy, who hung on to her for a long time. "You can do this, Cissy," were Bridget's parting words.

Later in the car, Michael turned abruptly to Bridget. "I told my mother I want to stay with you even after she goes back home. Is that okay?"

Bridget's heart leaped. "Of course, it's okay. We can make this work long term."

Having a teenager living with her was an adjustment for Bridget, but she was determined to make it work. Gone were the days when she stayed late at the office. If a deadline loomed, Bridget took the work home and finished it there. Gone also were the evening glasses of wine. She didn't think it right to drink in front of Michael, given his mother's struggles with alcohol.

Michael, for his part, was cooperative and helpful. He would wash the dishes after supper and never complained about Bridget's woeful attempts at cooking. He bravely ate whatever she prepared, but his appetite rejuvenated on Friday nights when he and Bridget went to Chip and Rosalina's for pizza with them and Matty.

One night, out of the blue, Michael announced he was taking cooking at school and had learned the basics. He asked his aunt if she would mind if he cooked. "Are you kidding? Even with your limited knowledge, you'll be better than I am. The kitchen is all yours."

"Thanks, Aunt Bridy. I'm happier than I've ever been."

Bridget choked back her emotion. "So am I."

Acknowledgments

Once again, I owe deep gratitude to Eileen O'Finlan, Author extraordinaire, and the writing group: Lee Baldarelli, Cindy Shinette, Rebecca Southwick, and Pam Reponen whose encouragement spurred me on to finish this book. And finally, to my publisher, Jessica Meltzer, who, once again, made it all possible.